THE LOTTERY ROSE

THE LOTTERY ROSE

IRENE HUNT

Margaret K. McElderry Books

New York London Toronto Sydney New Delhi

MARGARET K. McELDERRY BOOKS

An imprint of Simon & Schuster Children's Publishing Division

1230 Avenue of the Americas, New York, New York 10020

This book is a work of fiction. Any references to historical events, real people, or real places are used fictitiously. Other names, characters, places, and events are products of the author's imagination, and any resemblance to actual events or places or persons, living or dead, is entirely coincidental.

Text © 1976 by Irene Hunt

Cover illustrations © 2021 by Oriol Vidal

Cover design by Rebecca Syracuse © 2021 by Simon & Schuster, Inc.

MARGARET K. McELDERRY BOOKS is a trademark of Simon & Schuster, Inc.

For information about special discounts for bulk purchases, please contact Simon & Schuster Special Sales at 1-866-506-1949 or business@simonandschuster.com.

The Simon & Schuster Speakers Bureau can bring authors to your live event. For more information or to book an event, contact the Simon & Schuster Speakers Bureau at 1-866-248-3049 or visit our website at www.simonspeakers.com.

Also available in a Margaret K. McElderry Books hardcover edition

Interior design by Rebecca Syracuse

The text for this book was set in Minion Pro.

Manufactured in the United States of America

0221 OFF

This Margaret K. McElderry Books paperback edition March 2021

10 9 8 7 6 5 4 3 2 1

CIP data for this book is available from the Library of Congress.

ISBN 978-1-5344-7848-0 (pbk)

ISBN 978-1-5344-7847-3 (hc)

ISBN 978-1-5344-8185-5 (ebook)

THE LOTTERY ROSE

ONE

He bent over the book on his desk, hunching his shoulder blades together so that the partially healed cuts on his back would not be stretched apart, carefully keeping his shirt away from the raw wounds underneath, where even the slightest friction caused a burning pain.

He was seven and a half years old and although he had been in first grade for almost two years, he had not yet learned to read. The open book on his desk, however, was the one thing in school that he loved. On two occasions he had tried to steal it.

"I lost it," he had answered the school librarian

when she questioned him. He had learned to lie without blinking.

"No, Georgie, you took it home with you because you like it so much," Ellen Ames said calmly. "Bring it back to the library and I'll let you check it out as often as you wish. One of our rules is that a book can only be checked out for two weeks, but since this book means so much to you—" She did not finish her sentence. Georgie knew that Miss Ames was one of the few people in school who liked him.

The book was made up of page after page of brightly colored flowers, many of which Georgie recognized because sometimes Miss Ames sat beside him in the library and helped him pronounce the names of the different flowers. There were bushes full of red hibiscus blooms, and golden allamanda which reminded Georgie of little faces peeping from the glossy leaves around them; there was bright ixora—hedge after hedge full of orange clusters seeming not to mind the heat of Florida sunlight in the least; and there were masses of tangled carissa holding up tiny white blooms which looked, Miss Ames told him, a good deal like the snowflakes she had once seen flying down from the sky when she lived in a strange place called up north.

Finally there came the pages Georgie loved most,

those glowing with roses, thousands of them, bushels and tons of roses so beautiful that he ached to be among them, maybe to whisper to them if there was no one around to make fun of a boy who loved flowers. As he looked at these pages, Georgie's fears left him for a few safe minutes; he was able as he stared at the roses to draw a long breath and to feel something quiet and good stealing all through his body. His mother and Steve seemed to get lost in his thoughts, so did all the kids in the classroom. So did Miss Cressman.

Miss Cressman didn't like Georgie much. She got mad at kids who didn't know the words she pointed to when she wrote a long list on the blackboard; she got especially mad at Georgie because he played hooky and lied and set fires.

Once he set a fire under Miss Cressman's new car and there was a big row in the principal's office with the principal and Miss Cressman and later the police, all yelling at Georgie and trying to make him say yes, that he had done it and getting madder every minute because he wouldn't say it and they couldn't prove that he was lying.

After that day, Georgie got so mean that Miss Cressman moved his desk away to the back of the room where he couldn't bother the other kids, and sometimes the whole day would go by when she wouldn't say a word to him or even try to make him learn to read. On those days he could look at his book hour after hour and love the pictures of flowers and feel safe.

One day, though, when the class had kind of a game instead of work, Georgie closed his book and listened to what the others were saying. Miss Cressman asked all the children to think of something they liked best and then to talk about it to the others. She asked one kid after another and sometimes she even laughed a little at the things they said. She might have skipped Georgie altogether as she pointed around the room, but one girl said, "Miss Cressman, you forgot to ask Georgie what he likes," and so Miss Cressman asked him, as she did the others.

There had been all kinds of answers about the things the kids liked best. One of them thought the smell of gasoline was nice, and one girl thought the feel of a kitten's fur was the best thing that she knew. Someone liked the sound of an air-conditioner whirring away on a hot night, and one boy said his favorite thing was the taste of beer left in glasses after his parents and their friends had finished a card game.

Georgie was afraid to answer when Miss Cressman

pointed to him, but he did, after a few seconds and in a very low voice while he stared down at his desk.

"I like flowers," he said, blushing because he guessed that mean people were not supposed to like things that were nice. Then when the kids saw him blush, they giggled the way they always did when he couldn't read the primer stories or say the words Miss Cressman wrote on the board.

Georgie put his head down on his desk and tried to drown out the sound of giggles by holding his hands against his ears. He wished that Miss Cressman would say, "You mustn't laugh at Georgie," the way she told them they mustn't laugh at Alfie when he stuttered, but she didn't. She didn't care if they laughed at him because he was dumb and mean and set a fire under her car. He didn't care whether Miss Cressman liked him or not, but strangely a small sigh forced itself up from his chest and Georgie raised his head and looked at her.

He was scarred by a deep burn on the left side of his head which left him partly bald, with a crumpled ear and a streak that looked like fire running down the back of his neck. He didn't remember getting that burn; it had happened when he was still a baby.

His mother told him about the scar and crumpled

ear once when she had finished drinking all the whiskey from her last bottle on the shelf and was angry because there wasn't any more. It was when her whiskey was gone that Rennie Burgess hated her child most.

"You was yellin' that day, Georgie, 'til you drove me and Steve nearly crazy. So Steve said he'd give you somethin' to yell about—and he did. He give you plenty to yell about." She looked at Georgie and made her eyes narrow as she spoke. "Steve didn't like it that I was saddled with you when he took me for his girl-friend so he ain't ever been over-fond of you from the start. You and Steve ain't ever goin' to be close friends, Georgie—" She began laughing loudly at that and Georgie ran from her, rushing down the back stairs and hunting a hiding place among the garbage cans in the alley where he could sleep that night.

Steve came to the apartment every few weeks, sometimes staying only for the night; on other visits (and these were the terrible times) he brought a suit-case with him and stayed for several days. It was then that Georgie was apt to be half-starved after being tied in a closet without food, sometimes for a day, some-times for two or even three days. His eyes were always blackened when he returned to school, provided Steve allowed him to return, and his forehead was usually crisscrossed with raw stripes made by Steve's belt.

There were deeper cuts and welts hidden underneath his shirt. When the school nurse first discovered them, she made Georgie take her home with him to see his mother. There was a lot of yelling that day; Georgie's mother almost collapsed as she talked to the nurse, screaming that she was a hard-working widow trying to raise a boy who had made nothing but trouble for her since the day he was born. But, she added, she had never lifted a hand against him; the welts and bruises on his back had been made by a gang of big kids in the neighborhood who made it a practice to beat up on smaller children.

Georgie himself was silent when he was questioned, only shaking his head and staring past his questioners. The school librarian had taken him aside sometimes when his battered appearance was worst.

"Who hurt you, Georgie?" Miss Ames had asked, but he wouldn't answer. "Were you in a fight as your mother says you were?" she asked finally and he nodded, glad that she had given him a chance to slide out of further questioning.

That became his only answer to any inquiries about his hurts: "Got in a fight with some big kids," he would reply, and although there were people in the apartment building where he lived who knew better, nothing was ever done about it.

He had been taught from his earliest years to feel a deadly fear of what would happen if he ever told on Steve. "He'll kill you, Georgie," Rennie Burgess told her son when he was hardly more than a baby, and she repeated her warnings over and over from that time on. "Steve's not goin' to stand for a kid whinin' on him. He'll kill you if you ever say anything against him so you be smart, Georgie. You keep your mouth shut about Steve."

Fear of Steve was never completely out of Georgie's mind; awake or asleep, it was always there, but it was furthest removed when he sat quietly in his seat, far in the back of the room away from other children, and looked at the book Ellen Ames allowed him to keep week after week in spite of any rule. There were no people in the pictures and Georgie liked that; a few people were sometimes kind, but most of them were dangerous. But a world of flowers and trees, fields and woods and quiet rivers brought a comfort to him which allowed him to smile to himself, helped him to become deaf to Miss Cressman's voice. One of the pictures he loved best was in soft green and it reminded him of when the gray fog rolled in across the Florida scrub, and color met with moist air, the two of them swirling together until color and wetness became one and the same. He wondered if he might not be able to hide in the misty green of such a place, and the prospect brought a lonely wave of wishfulness to him. Georgie stared at the picture and tried to imagine the comfort of being safely hidden from his mother and Steve in the fog and greenness.

Pictures from the book were ones to keep in his mind when he burrowed far down into his bed at night, covering his head with the sheet. His bed was the safest place in the apartment since Steve seldom bothered to look for Georgie when the boy was out of sight. It was hearing Georgie's shrill cry of fear that caused Steve to take off his belt and bring it down fiercely upon Georgie's back. And so Georgie tried desperately to keep out of Steve's sight, sometimes in the alley back of the apartment building, sometimes curled like a snail, as small as he was able to make himself, under the sheet on his bed. To have pictures from the flower book in his mind during the hours of darkness, to have something good to think about while his mother and Steve laughed together or fought and screamed at one another—this was something that was important.

His joy in looking at a page of full-blown roses

in his book was brought to a sudden end when Miss Cressman stopped at his desk to scold him for not attempting to do the assigned pages in his workbook. He stared at her for a second as if he did not recognize her, then giving up his dream of peaceful gardens full of roses, he opened the reading workbook on his desk.

"You haven't tried, Georgie, you never try," Miss Cressman said. She pointed to a line of four pictures: a tree, a turtle, a train and a thimble. "Say the names of these pictures, Georgie; repeat them after me," she ordered. When he obeyed, she said, "Now place an X under the pictures that begin with the same sound."

Georgie looked at her and then turned toward the window. Outside, the sky was blue. If there were any flowers out there they would be turning their faces up to look at that blue sky. And it didn't make any difference, so far as he could see, whether the names of any pictures began with the same sound.

Miss Cressman was watching him. "Think, Georgie." Her voice began to grow shrill. "Which pictures should have an X placed under them? Now do a little thinking and get to work."

She walked down the aisle a short distance from him and Georgie seized the crayon on his desk. "Here are all your damn X's, Miss Cressman," he said to himself, and he made a heavy, angry X under every picture on the page.

When Miss Cressman came back to his desk a few minutes later, she picked up his book and, after a glance, tore his worksheet into shreds and crumpled them into a tight ball. Then she and Georgie glared at one another until, somehow, Georgie was the winner, because Miss Cressman finally looked away from him and seemed to study her hands before going back to her desk. Her hands were white with long, rosy nails that looked, Georgie thought, as if they would like to scratch a boy who couldn't read a single word the long nails pointed out to him. Georgie often thought of ways in which a long, rosy nail might suddenly be broken.

When the bell rang for noon intermission, he hurriedly got off the school ground and into the alley back of the building where he lived. There he kicked over a half-dozen garbage cans and yelled back to a woman who came out on one of the balconies and threatened to have the police come and haul Georgie off to jail. He shrugged at the woman's threats, but he kicked no more cans and slowly made his way down to the apartment where he lived.

At the entrance he was no longer the impudent boy

who had glared at Miss Cressman or yelled back at the woman in the alley; he was suddenly wary and frightened like a little animal that senses a return of danger. The beating he had taken from Steve the week before had been very close to a killing; another one might be more than he could endure. But the beating had resulted in one good since it caused Steve to run away from the apartment. Georgie's screams had aroused some of the neighbors enough to make them yell at Steve—threatening, as the woman on the balcony had threatened Georgie, to call the police. Steve, however, did not shrug at the threat and it was now six days since he had shown up at the apartment.

There was always the dread, however, that Steve might have returned while Georgie was in school, and so it was necessary to climb the steps stealthily and to listen at the door for a while before he turned the knob. The door was usually left open since Steve lost his key and had forbidden Georgie's mother to lock the door in case he arrived some night without notice.

Standing at the half-opened door, Georgie could hear no sound except his mother's heavy breathing as she lay asleep on the living-room sofa. It seemed that she was alone; still Georgie could not be certain and he tiptoed inside fearfully, peeping around corners into all the rooms and finally the screened porch at the back where his bed was kept. There was no sign of Steve, and Georgie had a feeling of weakness that came with his relief.

Coming into the living room again he looked at his mother where she lay with her mouth open, one hand on a half-emptied glass which she had set on the floor beside her. She wore a tattered bathrobe which was stained with coffee and burned in places where she had dropped a lighted cigarette. Her hair was uncombed and the sickness which came of too much drinking made the small, hot apartment a vile-smelling place that Georgie hated. He thought suddenly and wistfully of the pictures in his flower book, the quiet places and the cool, sweet smells he was sure would be there.

He hesitated to wake his mother. Sometimes when she was not worried about her supply of whiskey, she went into one of her crying spells and put on an act of loving him. At such times she insisted upon kissing Georgie, hurting his raw back with a grip that grew tighter as he tried to free himself.

It was necessary, though, to wake her and to ask for food. He hadn't had breakfast and she had been too far along with her drinking the night before to cook supper for him. He had found some cold cuts and dry bread on the kitchen counter last night; that had comforted his empty stomach for a while, but now there was nothing else to eat in the kitchen.

Her waking was much as he had feared it would be. She rolled over on her side, pulling him to her, weeping noisily as she ran her hand across the cuts on his back while she declared that Steve would never be allowed inside the apartment again, that he would never have another chance to hurt her boy. She seemed to forget the times that she had joined Steve in torturing him or had sat with a drink in her hand, not caring whether Georgie lived through the beating Steve was giving him or not. Georgie never hated her so much as he did on these occasions when she kissed and cried over him.

"You are a old liar," he thought bitterly, but he did not speak. He needed food and she was his only hope.

Rennie Burgess continued her blubbering promises to Georgie even after he pulled himself away from her. "If that brute ever comes back, if he ever dares to show his ugly face here again, Georgie, we'll call the police and have him pulled off to jail. There'll be just Mamma and her little boy here, just the two of us together. How we'll be able to live, I don't know, but we'll manage somehow. Mamma will have a new lock put on the front door and her boy won't ever need to be afraid again. We'll find some way to live without ever taking another cent from Steve—" She stopped at those words and looked thoughtfully at the bottle beside the sofa.

A shamed feeling built up inside Georgie as he looked at her. No other kid in Tampa, he supposed, had a mother like this one—he wished that he were big enough to run away and never see her again.

"Are we goin' to have something to eat?" he asked finally when his mother gave him a chance to speak.

She groaned and swayed slightly when she got to her feet. "Poor Mamma's not well, Georgie," she told him. "Mamma's not up to cookin' much." She pulled aside her pillow and took out a purse from which she shook a few bills and coins upon the sofa. Picking up a dollar bill, she put it into Georgie's hand.

"Here, my little love, here's the last of Mamma's money to buy something for her boy at the grocery. A can of pork and beans, maybe? Wouldn't that be good? Hurry, now, and if Mamma has the strength, she'll go out to the kitchen and make coffee. Watch the change, Georgie; there'll be little enough, but watch it and bring every cent home to Mamma—"

Georgie ran out of the apartment, rubbing his mouth to rid it of the moisture left by her kisses.

The grocery store was only two blocks away, a

rundown place that for months had smelled unpleasantly of rotting vegetables and general filth. Lately, however, the store had undergone a thorough scrubbing and painting which gave it the look of an entirely different place. There was a new air of friendliness, too, under a changed management, and the lines of customers at the checking counter were longer than they had been in many months.

Georgie noticed that instead of the smell of vegetables rotting in the bins along the wall, there was a whiff of fresh paint when he stepped inside, and that the neat piles of lettuce and cauliflower and oranges looked clean and ready to eat. The new manager was all smiles, telling ladies, "Goodbye, ma'am, y'all have a nice day now"; he even had a friendly "Hello, there, little boy," for Georgie, who hardly ever bought anything more than a loaf of bread or a can of beans.

Georgie, however, made no reply to the manager's friendly greeting. Instead, he glowered and scuttled down another aisle out of the man's sight. Actually the manager had a rather mild-looking face, but he was tall and dark, and his height, his age, his dark complexion were, for Georgie, too much like Steve for comfort. The man's smiling words were lies, he was sure; lies like his mother's kisses and her calling Georgie "little love." He hated this man who made him think of Steve and he ran fearfully down the aisles, looking back to see that the manager was not following him.

At the canned goods section he found the beans he was looking for without difficulty and took them across the store to the lane where Mrs. Sims stood at her checker's station.

Mrs. Sims lived somewhere in Georgie's block and she was always kind; she asked too many questions— all of which Georgie refused to answer—but he admitted to himself that Mrs. Sims was nice. Once she had taken him to a movie for children at Christmastime and Georgie never forgot the wonder of it.

She smiled at him that morning when he came up to her station. "How are you, Georgie?" she asked, and he ducked his head slightly to indicate that he was all right. She looked at him thoughtfully for a time, and Georgie knew that she was wondering about the latest cuts and bruises on his face; she didn't ask about them though and he was glad of that.

She rang up the cost of his pork and beans and handed him his change. Then she tore a small piece of cardboard from a big roll beside the cash register and gave it to him.

"Look, Georgie, can you read numbers?" she asked.

He could. In fact he could add and subtract a little; it was just being dumb in reading that made Miss Cressman angry with him. That, and setting a fire under her car, and smelling bad because his mother never washed his clothes or said anything about taking a bath. But numbers, yes. If he could have been as good in everything else as he was in numbers, Miss Cressman might have smiled at him the way she did at the smart kids.

He was immediately interested in the row of numbers on the card Mrs. Sims had given to him. "I can say 'em easy, all of 'em," he said, and there was just a suggestion of a smile on his lips when he looked up at her.

"Well, then, let me tell you about these numbers." She took Georgie's hand and held it in both her own. "You see, the new manager is holding what we call a lottery next Saturday morning. If you're here at ten o'clock, you'll see him draw cards from that big kettle by the door. If one of the cards should happen to have the same numbers as the ones on this card I've given you, you would win a prize. How about that, Georgie?"

His face lighted up with sudden eagerness and Mrs. Sims's face took on a worried look almost immediately. "Now don't expect too much, Georgie. There are hundreds, maybe a thousand of these cards. Only a few people can be lucky. You may not win anything this time, but take the card anyway and be here Saturday morning."

Privately she made up her mind that there would at least be a candy bar in her pocket for him.

TWO

eorgie walked along the hot street changed from a child who had never known hope for tomorrow into one who suddenly had gained, not just hope, but a bright certainty within him, and it was delicious and sweet. Mrs. Sims's warning that he might not win anything had by-passed him completely; he had only heard the possibility of winning a prize if the numbers on his ticket matched certain others on Saturday morning. That was enough. He knew that he would win, he believed he had actually won already, that somewhere in that store there was a package that no one but Georgie Burgess could claim. The row of numbers on the cardboard ticket were magic. They wouldn't fail him.

He forgot about being hungry and when his mother wakened fretfully up to his return and told him that she was too sick to bother with fixing a lunch for him, he set the can of beans aside for supper and got out of the apartment as quickly as he could.

There was a park a few blocks away with a lagoon shaded on one side by a cluster of Australian Pines where he could be alone with his ticket and its magic numbers. He wouldn't go back to school this afternoon. He would have a long dream while he sat hunched against one of the trees, a long afternoon of stillness during which he would repeat the line of numbers as he looked up into the scraps of sky showing through the trees. He lost himself after a while in the wonder those numbers were going to create for him, repeating them over and over, making them into a little crooning song.

"8662 dash 71 dash 4923," he sang, never knowing that at school his record read "mentally challenged" and that mentally challenged children were almost never able to remember a line of ten numbers long enough to repeat them.

Neither did it occur to him that the card with all the numbers actually belonged to his mother since it was her dollar that had been used to buy the beans. Such a detail would not have impressed him even if it had been pointed out. The card was his, the numbers were his friends, his alone, and the prize when he received it on Saturday morning would be his. He shivered at the prospect. What kind of prize it would be didn't really matter. Anything. A prize could be anything. Winning it with numbers that were his, numbers from his own particular scrap of cardboard, numbers that nobody else in the entire city could claim—that was a prospect that made his dream as bright as the sunlit pages in his flower book. He closed his eyes and drew his dream close about him, burrowing into it as he burrowed under the sheet on his bed at night to find a feeling of safety and peace.

It was not long, however, until problems began to take shape in his mind and his dream became troubled. Steve would be sure to scream that Georgie was a thief and had stolen the prize from some neighborhood store. Georgie felt a sharp pain growing inside him. Steve had once beaten him for taking a piece of bread without asking for it; now a prize, something sure to be beautiful and costly, would touch off a rage in Steve that could well be worse than anything Georgie had yet known. He began to feel sick. The beating would be bad enough, but Steve would either destroy the prize or keep it for himself. He had killed a kitten that Georgie once carried home; he had kept for himself a box of colored pencils after he had beaten Georgie for stealing them at the dime store. To win a prize and then to have Steve take it from him would be unbearable. Georgie's face was anxious and drawn by the time evening came and he prepared to go home. He looked like a small old man, hopeless with worry.

He felt his worries dimming, however, in the days that followed. Steve stayed away from the apartment for the rest of the second week, and that in itself lifted some of the terror from Georgie's life, giving him hope that he could do something with his prize on Saturday without either his mother or Steve knowing anything about it. He slept in his porch bedroom, bolting the door each night although he knew that no bolt could keep Steve outside if he chose to come in.

His mother soon set up a wailing that they were out of money and Georgie knew what that meant—Steve and the few dollars he flung at her upon his return would be welcome. She looked at her son, openly angry that his bruises and scars had in a weak moment wrung from her the promise that Steve would not be tolerated if he showed up again. It was getting to be time for his return since he seldom stayed away more than three weeks at a time, and she made it plain to Georgie in a pouting whine that they must have the money Steve gave her.

"Look, Georgie, my old man flogged me when I was a kid your age. Plenty of times I got beat up 'til I was raw. You ain't the only one that's had leather laid on you. And you bring a lot of it on yourself, Georgie. You start to scream as soon as you look at Steve and that irks him. Naturally, it irks him. And when Steve is irked he's like my old man used to be—he just naturally starts to think about givin' a screamin' kid a good lickin'." She poured herself another glass of whiskey and sat looking at Georgie thoughtfully.

"Havin' you around has caused me a lot of trouble, Georgie. I could of done things different if I hadn't had you on my hands. So you just make up your mind to it—if you expect to eat, you're goin' to have to live with Steve now and then or keep out of his way. Facts are facts, Georgie. If we don't have Steve, we ain't goin' to eat or"—her eyes measured the amount of whiskey left in the last bottle—"we ain't goin' to eat—or nothin'—"

Georgie withdrew from the sound of her voice as quickly as he could. In his porch bedroom a street lamp threw enough light for him to study the ticket and the numbers on it. "8662 dash 71 dash 4923," he whispered to himself. Then he put his hands over the numbers and named them from right to left—"3294 dash 17 dash 2668." He smiled to himself. They were his forever, even if he sometime lost the ticket, the numbers were his, written somewhere inside his brain.

On Saturday morning while his mother slept, Georgie stole out of the apartment and was at the grocery store a full hour before the drawing. Mrs. Sims saw him standing outside, his face pressed against the window. She suddenly looked sad and worried.

At ten o'clock the store manager went over to the bucket beside the door and after stirring and tossing the pile of tickets in it, he chose a little girl from the crowd around the store's entrance, blindfolded her, and instructed her to draw out twelve tickets which he counted loudly as she placed them one by one in his hand. Then going to the window he wrote the winning numbers on a white sheet of paper while the crowd gaped and a few early winners screamed.

Georgie had gone over to stand close at Mrs. Sims's side when the drawing began and he pressed his ticket into her hand. Mrs. Sims took it, fumbling in her pocket for the candy bar she had put there to ease Georgie's disappointment a little.

Then it happened and Mrs. Sims gasped. One line of numbers flowing along with the manager's thick black crayon on the big sheet of white paper suddenly became, not just any numbers, but Georgie's magic line of them, which read 8662—71—4923.

At first, Georgie thought Mrs. Sims didn't believe that the numbers on his card matched the ones in the window. She read both rows again and then she pointed to each number on the card as she read the ones in the window. Finally she gave the ticket to Georgie and asked him to call out the numbers slowly. "I have to be sure that my eyes aren't playing tricks," she told him.

When she was certain she sat down weakly on a chair near her station and beckoned the boy to her. "You've won, Georgie," she told him quietly. She was awed. There was something about this one chance in thousands happening to a boy like Georgie that made her hands tremble as she drew him to her side.

"What do I get?" Georgie whispered, his eyes shining.

"I don't know. Something nice, I'm sure."

The first prize was a plastic canister set that went to a woman who seemed very pleased with it; the second was a giant-sized box of detergent that went to another woman who shrugged a little, but put the big box in her cart with the other groceries she had bought. Next there was an aluminum saucepan which a pretty girl pushed resentfully aside when it was awarded to her number, and then a glass salad bowl with a wooden fork and spoon for a young woman who tried to pick it up and at the same time collect three small children who were racing around the store. After that there was a short blue kitchen apron decorated with tulips around the hem for a huge man who grinned sheepishly as he folded his prize and placed it in the pocket of his jacket. Then the sixth prize was awarded and it went to the holder of the ticket numbered 8662—71—4923.

It was a rosebush, a slightly dried out rosebush wrapped in burlap with a card attached carrying instructions for planting and showing a picture of a full-blown scarlet rose, one of the dozens promised when the bush would finally bloom.

A rosebush. Of all good things on earth, a rosebush. The whole world set up a singing as Georgie clutched the prize against his chest. "The best prize in the world," he whispered to Mrs. Sims who closed her eyes as her mind raced through all the difficulties Georgie was bound to encounter in caring for this best prize in the world.

Lost in a frenzy of excitement Georgie ran from the store, bumping into people, stumbling once and falling flat, but the hurt of his fall didn't matter so long as the rosebush was not damaged. He heard some people laughing and one woman scolded him when he ran against her and sent a bag of groceries flying. Georgie paid no attention to any of them. He simply ran and ran, panting with the weight of the awkward bundle in his arms, a deep confusion beginning to spin in his brain.

The hot street was lined with shabby apartment houses, filling stations and decrepit-looking stores; there was hardly a stretch of grass to be seen, much less a garden where a rosebush could be planted.

The park where he often hid on days when he skipped school was beautiful enough for his prize, but it wouldn't do—the police wouldn't allow it to be planted there. The school playground was paved with asphalt, but there were a few plants near the entrance to the building. Georgie paused for a minute thinking of Miss Ames and the flower book, then pushed the idea that had occurred to him aside. Except for them the school was really a despised and threatening place, undeserving of the scarlet blooms the bush was sure to produce once it was planted and watered. Moreover, there was Miss Cressman who had no right even to look at his prize, and plenty of kids who would take delight in destroying a plant once they learned that it belonged to "dumb Georgie." He held the bush tighter in his arms and hurried past the school, wondering at himself for having ever thought of planting it there.

He did not know where to turn and so he simply ran on and on. Although it was only the first week of March the Florida sun was steaming hot, and sweat ran down Georgie's forehead into his eyes; it ran down his neck too, and stung sharply when it reached the sensitive flesh on his shoulders and back.

For endless blocks the city was a jungle of apartment buildings and paved streets. Later he entered a trailer-court area full of screaming children and yapping dogs. He hurried on and on, finally reaching a neighborhood of pretty houses and well-kept lawns. Once he came to a garden filled with bright flowers and there he stood and looked for a long time, almost determined to stop and ask a great favor, but he didn't, being fearful and uncertain.

A few houses farther on he had the chance to request a place for his rosebush. A woman, seeing him from her doorway, came out with a glass of cool orange juice and offered it to him. It was well after noon and he hadn't eaten all day; the juice gave him comfort and a new energy. When the woman inquired about his rosebush he came very close to asking if he might plant it on her lawn, but a sudden agony reminded him that he'd possibly never be able to find this house again, that leaving his prize here meant that he was giving it to a stranger.

And so he trudged on without a plan, without a hope of finding a suitable place for his plant where he could still be able to see it daily and to call it his own. He walked on because there was nothing else to do. After a while he sat down in the shadow of a white oak tree near the street's curb, all the happiness he had felt earlier flowing from him and leaving him exhausted and tearful.

After he had cried for a while he thought of Mrs. Sims and wondered why he had not asked her for help immediately. He had been so crazy with the excitement of winning a rosebush all his very own that he'd forgotten about her. Now, he realized the need for a plan of action.

He got up wearily but full of a new determination to go back and find Mrs. Sims. He would even bring himself to leave the bush with her for a while if it was necessary, long enough to give him time to think of what he might do, time, maybe, to plan how he could run away, where neither Steve nor his mother would ever find him or ever have a chance to see the dozens of red roses that he would pick each day from his bush. Mrs. Sims was the one person he could trust until his plans were made and so he hugged the bush closer to him and turned in what he hoped was the direction that would lead him back to the store.

At mid-afternoon, exhausted and hungry, he collapsed in a lot covered by clumps of palmetto and scraggly long-needled pines with new cones standing upright on the branches like green Christmas candles. Here he found shelter from the sun and here, once fast asleep, he dreamed and the dream was so peaceful and sweet that he smiled and, for a time, had not a care in the world.

The dream had its beginning in the flower book. Even in sleep, a part of Georgie's brain remembered the pictures and after a while the pictures became alive and he was able to walk through a field where the wind made a thousand flowers nod in the grass, from there into a dim, green forest and then at last into a garden where a rosebush suddenly appeared, safely planted and covered with a mass of scarlet blooms. There was sunlight touching every part of the dream, however; it was gentle sunlight, bright gold, but never burning like the kind that beat down on city streets at times and made a small apartment like an oven. Everywhere there was peace and stillness in his dream and Georgie had no fear of anyone finding or daring to hurt him. If the taunting kids in school, or Steve or Miss Cressman or his mother should appear, Georgie knew exactly what to do: he would close the book quickly, making the hard covers snap as they came together and hid the pictures inside. Then he would stand, not far away but out of their sight, and he would laugh at the angry faces of the enemies who were forbidden to enter a world that belonged only to Georgie Burgess.

When he finally wakened, he lay quietly thinking about his dream, half believing for a while that he had actually been away on a pleasant journey and was only now returning to the palmetto grove and to the troubles all around him. He noticed after a few moments that the air was cooler than it had been before his nap, that the sky was overcast with black clouds that meant the approach of a spring storm. He was grateful for the coolness and remembering his plan to find Mrs. Sims, he got to his feet feeling refreshed and hopeful.

Realizing now that his heedless rushing during the

earlier part of the day had been foolish, he resolved to be wiser about the return trip. He knew the name of the street he wanted, he made inquiries as he went along and slowly, very slowly, he began to recognize landmarks in the distance.

He had to stop and find shelter in the doorway of an empty store when the storm finally broke. It was a fiercely noisy storm, crackling with crooked streaks of lightning across the sky and roaring with peal after peal of thunder. The rain, when it started at last, came down in sheets so heavy that it blotted out the buildings only a few feet away, emptying a downpour of water that sank into the soil as if thousands of parched mouths beneath the surface were sucking it under.

The storm stopped suddenly after about a half hour, and Georgie set out again along the nearly deserted sidewalk. The darkness by now was deep enough for the car lights, that had been turned on because of the storm, to remain shining as the lines of traffic wavered like long glowing worms creeping cautiously along the slippery wet pavement.

By the time Georgie reached his home neighborhood, the city looked as if it were spread out in a great field of lights. Water from the flooded streets gurgled as it ran down through the sewers; the walls of apartment houses were checkered with lighted and darkened windows. Entrance halls opening on the street were mostly dark. Someone might be hiding in one of them, someone like Steve. Georgie hurried past the darkest ones. He knew that the grocery store would be closed by this time, that the place would be dark, that there would certainly be no chance of seeing Mrs. Sims before the next morning.

Pulling himself along he finally reached the school building standing huge in the wet darkness, all its windows black except when a passing car made some of them flash with gold for a second. Then he took his usual short cut through the alleys and came at last to the entrance of the building in which there was an apartment that was neither a home nor a place of real safety, but it was the one spot in all the city where he had a chance to find a little food and a bed.

He climbed the stairs and, as always, listened for a minute outside the door. There was no sound inside; every room was dark and so still that he decided his mother must be alone. He hoped so.

When he entered the living room, the door creaked a little in spite of his great care in opening it and at the sound a light was snapped on. Georgie could see his mother, sprawled as usual on the sofa fast asleep, and Steve moving uncertainly as he got out of the only armchair in the room.

Georgie gave a shrill scream of terror and as his mother had told him many times, that made Steve crazy-mad.

She was right. Georgie's scream made Steve crazy-mad that night.

THREE

When Georgie regained consciousness the dimly lighted apartment seemed to be full of people. The first person he saw was a young woman in a nurse's uniform who leaned over him as he lay on the sofa, bathing his head and neck, laying soft bandages across his wounds. He gave a choking gasp as he realized where he was and tried to get up, looking wildly about the apartment to see if Steve lurked somewhere in the shadows. The nurse spoke to him quietly and made him lie down again.

"Don't try to get up," she told him. "It's all right now—they're both gone, the man and woman too."

She touched his shoulder gently. "Lie still. We mustn't put any pressure on this arm."

Two men came in from a group of neighboring tenants who stood in the kitchen. One was the janitor of the building; the other was a young police officer, so young an officer that he looked hardly more than a boy. Only a few weeks on his job, this was his first experience with child abuse and what he had seen left him a little white around the mouth.

The janitor was sweeping up glass and splintered furniture; the police officer was writing on a pad of paper. "I'd like to talk to the boy before I leave." He made a questioning gesture toward the nurse. "Is it all right? Can he talk now?"

She nodded. "I still have more wounds to dress before you take him to Children's Hospital. His left arm is broken. You'll have to question him, though I'm afraid he's still confused."

The young policeman came over and sat beside the sofa. "Your name is Georgie Burgess, the janitor tells me. Is that right?"

Georgie's lips formed a yes weakly. He stared at the young man.

"And this man who beat you—what is his name?"

Rennie Burgess's warnings sounded in her son's

ears: "You ain't hurt too bad, Georgie. You get over your lickin's soon enough. But if you ever tell on Steve, you'll be hurt like you ain't ever dreamed about. Steve won't stand for any kid tellin' on him—"

Georgie shuddered at the question. "I—I just got in a fight with some big kids—"

The policeman looked at him for a long time. Finally he said, "I see. But the janitor and some of the men in this building came up here and found him beating you with the leg of a chair. Do you remember that?"

Georgie didn't answer. The policeman continued, "Who is this man?"

"Don't know," Georgie muttered. That was true. He had no idea who Steve really was, where he lived when he wasn't with Georgie's mother, or how he earned the money he gave her.

"Is he your father?" the policeman asked.

"I don't think I got a father."

"This woman—this Rennie Burgess—" the young man flipped through some of the pages he held. "She's your mother?"

"I—I guess so."

"I don't blame you for doubting it," the policeman said in a low voice. He was silent then, watching the nurse wash blood and hair from a deep wound on Georgie's scalp.

"Do you see much of this?" he asked her after a while.

"Much," she answered, "and not always in the slums either."

The janitor spoke up from the doorway. "Them two ought to be held li'ble for the damage they done around here tonight—half-killin' the kid and breakin' up ever'thing in the place when they started fightin' us because we come in. I don't know when I've had to clean up so much junk. I've emptied four cans down the chute already—"

A sudden memory caused Georgie to cry out. "My prize," he screamed. "Where's my rosebush?" He turned from the nurse to the police officer, his eyes imploring each of them to help him.

"Did you see a rosebush around here?" The nurse turned to the janitor quickly.

"I seen a bunch of dry sticks that might of been a rosebush. Is that what he's hollerin' about?"

Georgie tried to get up again, but the nurse held him down firmly. He turned pleading eyes to her. "Make him give it to me, lady. I won it at the grocery store. It's mine; make him give it to me."

"That kid's out of his head," the janitor said sullenly. "I'm not goin' through all that junk for no bunch of trash he's dragged home from the grocery store."

"I think you'd better find his rosebush," the nurse said crisply. She looked at the two men, her lips pressed closely together. The policeman got up and walked toward the janitor.

"Show me where you dumped it," he said.

Georgie sobbed as he and the nurse waited. He hadn't cried when she washed his wounds, not even when she lifted his broken arm and it had hurt terribly. "I didn't steal it," he told her between sobs. "Honest, I didn't. I had a ticket and the numbers on it matched. You can ask Mrs. Sims."

"Who is Mrs. Sims, Georgie?"

"The checker at the grocery. She'll tell you I won it at the store."

"Yes, I believe you. We'll talk to Mrs. Sims after a while. The police want to talk to all the people around here who know you."

The policeman returned about ten minutes later, a battered plant in his hands.

"Is this your rosebush, Georgie?" he asked, holding it toward the boy.

"Yes. Yes, it's my prize." Georgie seized the plant

with his right hand and held it tightly within the curve of his arm. Unmindful of the thorns, he buried his face against it in a spasm of love and relief.

The policeman watched him for a moment and then shook his head slowly. "My good God Almighty," he said in a low voice.

The next several days were a blur in Georgie's mind. He had a low fever which wouldn't leave, and that with the pills needed for bearing the pain of his injuries, kept him only partly conscious of what was happening around him. He knew that doctors examined his hurts and took many X-ray pictures of his head and back, that nurses changed his dressings each day and that one nurse took the time to sprinkle water on the peatmoss surrounding the roots of his rosebush. At night he slept with his good right arm hanging down beside his bed, his hand touching his prize.

When he was a little better he had a visit at the hospital from Mrs. Sims. "I've been here before, but always when you were asleep and the nurses thought I shouldn't wake you up," she said. He noticed that her face looked happy.

"The court is letting me be a foster mother to you, Georgie, until they've found a place for you. I wish I could keep you always, but at least I can take you home with me this afternoon and say that you're my boy for a little while."

Georgie had no idea who the court might be or what Mrs. Sims meant by the words foster mother, and he was too tired to ask or to care very much so long as no one said that he must go back to the apartment where he had lived with his mother.

Mrs. Sims and her husband were kind to him, but Georgie and his rosebush were left alone each day while his foster parents worked at their jobs and when he began to sleep a little less, the days grew lonely. Sometimes at night, the three of them talked about what they could do about his bush.

"There's no place around this building where we can plant it, Georgie," Mrs. Sims told him, "but a man down at the florist's shop says the bush will stay healthy for a long time if we keep the moss around it well watered. And maybe in a week or two we'll be able to find a place where we can give it a bed in some yard or garden."

Once Georgie overheard some whispers between Mrs. Sims and her husband. He wouldn't have paid any attention except that he suddenly realized they were talking about his mother and Steve.

"They say his mother ain't long to live. Too much whiskey over the years," he heard Mrs. Sims say. "The man's in jail. Judge O'Neill has talked to all the neighbors, the police and people over at the school. Now he wants to see Georgie himself—they'll let us know when we're to take him over—"

"I wish we could keep him," Mr. Sims said after a while. "If we were younger—and if we had the money. As it is we're in no shape to take on a youngster—" They were both silent after that and Georgie was left wondering.

A few days later Mrs. Sims stayed home from work. "A social worker is coming to take us to court today—the judge wants to talk with you. Try to answer his questions in a polite way, Georgie—don't just duck your head. Try to remember that, won't you?"

Georgie's eyes were wide with fright. "What's a judge?" he asked.

"This one's a good man, I hear. He wants to do what's best for you, Georgie. You needn't feel afraid; he just needs to know you better."

On the day they went to court a tall woman who called herself a social worker pushed Georgie in a wheelchair down a long hall which seemed to him to go on and on for at least a mile with dozens of closed doors on either side. When they finally opened one of the doors, a lady showed them into another room where a man with thick eyebrows sat at a desk and motioned them to sit near him. He extended a hand toward Georgie.

"I am Judge O'Neill, Georgie, and I know a great deal about the things that have happened to you. I have some plans for you though, some pretty good ones, I think. We must talk them over." He paused and studied Georgie's face thoughtfully. Finally he smiled. "They tell me that you have a rosebush that you like a lot," he said.

Georgie nodded. He wondered who would have told this stranger about his prize.

"I am a rose fancier myself, Georgie; that means that I grow roses and try to learn all I can about caring for them. I can understand how eager you are to get your bush planted and so I've found a place out in the country for you where some very nice people will take care of both you and your bush."

Georgie just stared at him, knowing he'd have to say all right. Grown-up people could do anything they wanted to do.

"This place I have in mind is a school where you will live—where you'll eat and sleep and learn, where the people who have been cruel to you can never hurt you again. It's a very good school—"

The word school made Georgie gasp. "Couldn't I stay with Mrs. Sims?" he managed to ask.

"I'm afraid not. Mrs. Sims and her husband can't very well take care of you. Anyway, I think you should be taken far out of your old neighborhood—" Judge O'Neill was silent for a short time and then continued in his deep voice. "This school is for boys most of whom have lost one or both parents though some of them are sent there by both parents simply because it is a good place for boys to learn and at the same time be healthy and happy. The lady in charge is one of the finest teachers I have ever known. You'll like her. She is a tiny little woman about this high—" He lifted his hand to a point just a few inches above the back of his chair. "You'll call her Sister; her full name is Sister Mary Angela."

Georgie's head drooped and he made no reply. The judge reached out a hand and patted the boy's knee. Then he spoke to the social worker.

"I've managed to convince the Board of Directors that they can afford to take him for three months without tuition. After that I think we can get someone to sponsor the boy if he fits into the school—especially if Sister Mary Angela wants to keep him. I'm confident that this is the place for him—"

He shook hands with Georgie then, and wished him good luck. "Sister Mary Angela will find a place for your rosebush, too, Georgie. I've told her about it and she says 'No problem.'"

Georgie sighed deeply. He was reassured—he would be safe from Steve, he wouldn't have to be hungry or sleep in the alley; best of all, the rosebush would have a home. But in spite of that he felt an emptiness, a bewilderment about what was happening to him. That night he lay awake and stared into the darkness, wondering and worrying and becoming more and more afraid.

When plans were made to drive Georgie out to the school, Mrs. Sims put in a plea to ride along. "I want to know what the place is like—I want to see the people he'll be with," she explained earnestly. "If this place don't work out for Georgie, maybe we can take him. I don't know. I just don't know how we'd manage, but I can't sleep the night through 'til I know things are goin' to be all right for him—"

And so the three of them—Mrs. Sims, the social worker, and Georgie left for the school one bright spring morning. Georgie sat alone in the back seat of the car with the rosebush at his feet and watched the highway wind between woods and rivers and orange groves, through little towns with white roofs reflecting the glare of sunlight, along sandy beaches where blue water lapped endlessly and gulls circled and sped away like miniature silver jets diving through the sky.

They reached the school shortly after noon. It was a wide, rambling building of pale pink brick with dozens of white window facings and a roof of red tile. The social worker thought the green lawn with the white statue of a lady and her child under the shade trees made a lovely picture; the building itself, however, she thought was very ugly—a monstrosity, she said, and Mrs. Sims agreed with her. Georgie didn't know. He supposed it was ugly. All schools were, so far as he was concerned.

It was in the midst of a wide countryside with woods back of it and a bright river shining in the distance. Across the street, which was actually an unpaved lane bordered by a low curb, was the only other building to be seen. It was a large white, two-story house with green shutters and a green roof to match. It was much more beautiful, the two ladies in the front seat thought, than the school.

"The school was a women's college when it was first built," the social worker explained to Mrs. Sims. "The big house across the way had been the president's home. I've heard that it was bought two or three years ago by Paul Harper, a well-known writer who was killed in a car accident last year. His wife, Judge O'Neill tells me, was an actress in and around New York City. It seems they moved down here because of a mentally challenged child—"

When Georgie and his companions walked up the wide flight of concrete steps to the front entrance of the school, they were met by a tiny woman with a pretty face and great dark eyes that laughed one minute and were filled with a deep gentleness the next. She wore a white dress and a short veil set far back on her hair and held in place by a white band. Some strands of hair had settled themselves across her forehead and were plastered there by the damp, midday heat.

"I am Sister Mary Angela," she said in greeting, and after shaking hands with the two women she turned and took Georgie's hand. "I'm glad you're here, Georgie, both you and your rosebush. Judge O'Neill called to ask if we could find a good place for you to plant it and I told him you could choose any one of a half dozen places. We'll give the bush a sprinkle of water and then you can put it outside your window for the night."

Georgie ducked his head in spite of Mrs. Sims's urgings that he break this particular habit, and he could think of nothing to say. He was frightened and uneasy as he stood with the three women, especially when he heard Mrs. Sims say in a low voice, which she might have known he could overhear, "He's not had much home life, Sister. He's picked up some careless habits—bad table manners and forgetfulness about taking a bath. He may, once in a while say some words that will shock you—"

Sister Mary Angela laughed. "I am well acquainted with the ways and words of little boys from city streets, Mrs. Sims. I don't go into shock easily—"

When they were seated in the front parlor she rang a bell on a nearby table and a moment later a young nun came into the room. When Sister Mary Angela had introduced her to the two women, she led Georgie to the newcomer. "Sister Monica will take you to the dining room for a bite of lunch, Georgie, and then she will get one of the boys to show you around the playground. We'll call you before your friends leave."

Georgie walked with Sister Monica down the hall to the dining room without speaking. She seemed to understand that he didn't want to talk, and after an attempt or two, she gave up trying to start a conversation. She smiled though as she placed a sandwich and a glass of milk before him. Later she called a red-haired boy from the playground and put Georgie in his charge.

"Georgie is our new boy, Timothy—the one Sister asked you to look after for a while. Will you show him around the playgrounds and the vegetable gardens— maybe later he'd like to watch the baseball game the older boys are playing this afternoon."

"Sure. Sure, Sister, I'll show him around." The boy called Timothy was pleasant; some of the older boys were not.

"Hello, Ugly," one of them yelled at Georgie when Sister Monica was out of sight. Another one threw a pebble at the cast on Georgie's arm. "Who beat the hell out of you, Ugly?" he asked.

"Don't pay no attention to them," Timothy said, scowling. "They think they're big shots because they're thirteen, but wait and see how fast they get kicked off the team if Sister Monica hears them wise-cracking."

Georgie didn't answer. He was accustomed to names being yelled at him. When these kids learned that he couldn't read—then there would be other names. He knew them all, but he was too tired for caring. Anyway he had caught a glimpse of a flower garden across the street, and without a word, he started across the playground toward it.

It was as beautiful as any picture in the book he had loved, as bright and colorful as the garden in the dream he'd had that afternoon in the palmetto grove. And this was real—neither a picture nor a dream, but a wide mass of hedges, trees and flower beds that were almost within reach of his hands, all of them in bloom and in every color Georgie could imagine. The flowers sent waves of fragrance across the street to Georgie, fragrance that made him dizzy with its sweetness. He hoped frantically that this was one of the places Sister Mary Angela had in mind.

"Who does it belong to?" he asked Timothy just above a whisper.

"Her," Timothy answered and pointed across the lane toward a young woman who was busy at a distant flower bed. She was a tall lady with two long braids of blond hair that fell over her shoulders.

"That's Mrs. Harper," Timothy continued. "She's pretty all right, but she don't like us much. If we happen to knock a ball over there, we have to ask one of the Sisters to get it for us." Timothy paused and then decided to go on in spite of the fact that Georgie seemed to be paying little attention to what his guide was saying.

"You see, she had a boy named Paul, and he was a nice kid—all of us liked it when his dad brought him over to play ball with us. But one day some man didn't stop at a red light and Paul and his dad got killed. There's a grandfather that lives over there, and he's a real good guy—sometimes he comes over and reads out loud to us. And there's a little boy that ain't right up here—" Timothy put a forefinger to his temple. "He's cute, though, and we'd like to go over, some of us would, and play with him. But NO! A big fat NO! Mrs. Harper would scalp us bald if we went over there."

Georgie barely heard Timothy's words. The garden grew more beautiful with each passing moment and he realized that here was where his rosebush must be planted. After all his worry and searching he had found the perfect place for his prize.

That evening after Georgie had said goodbye to Mrs. Sims and the social worker, he went into the dining room with Timothy and sat beside him at one of the many round tables where a group of boys near his age ate together. There was a great deal of laughing among them, a cautious kicking of neighboring shins underneath the table, occasionally a pellet of pressed bread crumbs was sent flying across the dishes straight into the face of someone directly opposite. Once one of the boys asked Georgie about the cast on his arm, but Sister Monica happened along about that time and gave the questioner a certain kind of look.

"That meant shut up," Timothy explained in a low voice after talking had again been resumed around the table. "She told us this afternoon that we're not supposed to ask things about how another guy looks, but some of these clowns can't mind their own business." Timothy shrugged his shoulders and Georgie was grateful that the boys ignored his cuts and bruises during the remainder of the meal.

As twilight grew deeper Timothy told Georgie that they must go into the chapel for something he called vespers. "It's just some guys singin' while Sister Mary Angela plays the organ. When that's over we say a prayer or two—afterward we can raise the roof 'til bedtime. We don't always want to go, but we got to do it, no matter if we're Catholic or not—" He grinned at Georgie in a friendly way. "You meet me at that big door yonder when you hear a little bell ring, and we'll go in together—"

At the sound of the bell, however, Georgie slipped out of doors. There wasn't another boy in sight, not a nun, not anyone to disturb him. He took his rosebush from under his window, and hurried out to the curb where he could look across at the wonderful garden.

After a long time when the evening was almost night he saw Sister Mary Angela coming toward him.

She picked up a low stool from the lawn and seated herself upon it beside him. He thought maybe she'd be mad about the thing called vespers, but she didn't say anything about it.

"I've been wanting to talk to you about your rosebush, Georgie," she said in a friendly voice. "We'd better get it planted tomorrow, hadn't we?"

He wouldn't look at her. "Where?" he asked.

"How about just outside your room on the first floor? You'd be near it—you could see it the last thing before you go to sleep and the first thing in the morning. Wouldn't that be a good place?"

"No," Georgie answered.

"Where would you like to plant it then?"

"In the garden."

"You mean that garden?" she asked, pointing across the street.

"Yes."

"We can't, Georgie. That is not our garden and the lady who owns it is very strict about forbidding any of our boys to be over there." Sister Mary Angela stared over at the garden and her face grew sober, as if she had many thoughts in her mind. "You see, Georgie," she said after a while, "Mrs. Harper and her husband made that garden beautiful again after it had been neglected for a long time. It was something they both loved and it helped them to forget the homesickness they felt for their home in New York and for their old friends. Now that her husband is dead it reminds her of him. She would never allow us to plant a strange flower or bush in her garden—"

Georgie did not answer.

"Now let's think of a place over here," Sister Mary Angela continued. "I'll be proud to have a lovely rose somewhere on our grounds and to have you here so that you can take good care of it. Judge O'Neill will want to know how your bush is coming along—he may be able to drive out someday to see it—"

"The right place is over there," Georgie muttered, his head still lowered.

"Why is Mrs. Harper's garden more of a right place than dozens of others, Georgie?"

"It's like the garden in my book. My rosebush has to be there."

Sister Mary Angela pressed a hand against her temple as if her head ached. It was a while before she spoke, but when she did, her voice was very firm.

"I have to tell you, Georgie, that the answer is no. I will do all I can to make you happy, but your rosebush can't be planted over there."

Georgie raised his head and looked straight into her eyes. "If you won't let me, I won't plant it anywhere. Then it will die. And after that, I will die."

Sister Mary Angela sighed deeply as she got to her feet. "We must go inside now, Georgie—it's time that you were in bed. We'll talk about this again tomorrow—"

She held out her hand, but he drew away and walked silently beside her to the room she had prepared for him.

FOUR

The next morning Georgie was not able to eat his breakfast. Timothy noticed after a time that Georgie's food was untouched and that his eyes had a tired look in them.

"I guess you don't feel so good, huh, Georgie?" he asked as they walked away from the breakfast table together.

"I feel O.K.," Georgie answered. He knew that he didn't feel O.K., but he also knew that he didn't want to talk about his tiredness or his headache. He had other things to think about that morning.

Sister Mary Angela called for him to come to her

office in mid-morning. "Georgie, I've been thinking about the rosebush all night. Will you listen to what I am suggesting and try to understand?"

A sly plan began to take shape in Georgie's mind; it was not quite a lie—almost but not quite—and it would get Sister to stop talking about the rosebush until other plans came through.

"Yes, Sister," he said meekly and with so mild a face that she looked relieved.

"I've been thinking of so many possibilities for your bush—the entrance to our building at one side of the steps is one place where there is plenty of room and where every visitor would see and admire it—" She looked at Georgie hopefully.

"Yes, ma'am," he said.

Sister Mary Angela continued even more enthusiastically. "Then, of course, I've wondered why you and Timothy might not cultivate a flower garden together—a big plot to brighten up things in the midst of the boys' vegetable gardens. I'm pretty sure Timothy would be glad to take on such a project—he likes you, Georgie."

Georgie nodded slowly and Sister Mary Angela's eyes smiled at him.

"Of course I like the idea of the bush being right

outside your window, but then if you don't, we'll skip that possibility. But there's a very special place I'll give you if you want it—that's beside the statue of the Blessed Mother out under the Goldenrain trees in the comer of our lawn. Your rose would look lovely there, Georgie; red blooms against the white marble—can't you see them in your mind?"

Georgie looked at her with the unblinking look he had given Miss Ames when he lied about losing the book. "I'll have to think about these places, Sister—" He made his voice sound as if he agreed with much of what she had said.

"Of course. It would be foolish to decide in a rush. Why don't you look around at these places I've suggested? Take your time; the rosebush has waited this long—I guess another day or two won't matter."

He saw that Sister Mary Angela looked relieved, as he walked with her toward the door of her office. Then he went outside and made his plans for a visit to the house across the street.

He waited until afternoon when he saw the lady with the golden braids working in her garden beside a bent little man who, according to Timothy, was Old Eddie, Mrs. Harper's gardener. Georgie didn't quite have the courage to face the lady who might scalp a strange boy she discovered in her garden. He decided upon a less dangerous approach.

Only that morning he and Timothy had glimpsed a stout, brown woman busily wiping down some windows while an even stouter and younger woman sprawled in one of the lawn chairs and watched.

"That's Amanda," Timothy had said, pointing out the younger woman. "She's supposed to be the little boy's nurse, but I don't know—I think the grandfather is more of a nurse than she is. We call her 'Coca-Cola Amanda' because she drinks Cokes all day—that's why she's so fat, I guess—" Timothy laughed a little at his own gossip. "The other lady is Rosita—she's the house-keeper and she's Mexican. Rosita's all right—she bakes cookies for us sometimes—"

And so Georgie went first to see Rosita that after-noon.

She gasped slightly when she opened the kitchen door and saw Georgie with his rosebush. "My good-ness, little boy, whatever happened to you?" she asked. Then, she noticed the rosebush and her white teeth showed up nicely in her smile. "I don't think we need a rosebush right now," she told him.

"Could I talk to the lady that owns this garden?" Georgie asked timidly.

Rosita shook her head. "No, no, I don't think so. Mrs. Harper is very busy, and I'm pretty sure she'd not like it if we bothered her—" She stepped inside to a table and came out immediately with an iced cupcake in her hand. "Would you like this?" she asked kindly.

Georgie shook his head. "No, I don't feel like eatin'. When do you think I could talk to the lady out in the garden?"

Rosita's forehead folded into many wrinkles. "I don't know, child. You see, Mrs. Harper lost a boy about your age just a year ago—she—" Rosita shook her head and her face was sad, "she ain't up to talkin' much to other little boys right now—"

Georgie didn't move. He stood there, staring up at her, and his stare seemed to make Rosita nervous. "Why don't you go around in front to the screened porch? Mr. Collier is out there—he's our little boy's grandfather—Why don't you go around and speak to him?" she asked. Georgie had the feeling that she was anxious to be rid of him.

As he rounded the corner of the house, Georgie saw beyond the heavy iron gate at the edge of the lawn a sloping path that led down to a lake which lay sparkling like a looking-glass in the sunlight. There were trees here and there on both sides of the path, and halfway down to the lake there was a wide old tree like one he had often looked at in his flower book. Miss Ames told him once that it was a banyan tree, and he was pleased that he remembered the name.

When he found the porch, he knocked at the screen door and a man's pleasant voice asked him to come inside. The voice belonged to a slender old man with silver-gray hair and a beard that matched. He sat on a long chair with his feet stretched out before him and with pillows and books all around him. A small boy with curly blond hair and blue eyes that somehow looked lost and all alone sat close to the old man's side.

"Well, are you a peddler, young man? Are you selling rosebushes?" the man asked as soon as Georgie stepped inside.

Georgie shook his head. "I'm not sellin' it. I just want to plant it in your garden."

He noticed a worried look come over the old man's face, much like the look that came on Miss Ames's face when Georgie returned to school after a bad beating. He expected to hear the words so many people said when they looked at him for the first time—"What happened? Who hurt you?"

But the little boy's grandfather didn't ask the words Georgie expected. He seemed to be busy with some thoughts for a minute, then he smiled. "I'm afraid there isn't a chance of your planting the rosebush here. This garden belongs to my daughter and she's very particular about choosing the plants she wants in it. Anyway, shouldn't you plant it somewhere near you so you can tend it?"

"No, it has to be here. This is the right place for it."

"Maybe you haven't looked far enough. By the way, do you live at the school across the street?"

"I've lived there from yesterday."

"So you're a new boy. Do any of the Sisters know that you've brought your bush over here?"

"No." Georgie rested his awkward parcel on the terrazzo floor of the porch.

"Where did you find your bush then?" the grandfather asked after a pause.

"I didn't find it. I had a ticket that won it at a grocery store. It had some numbers on it that made them win the bush to me—"

Georgie changed the subject suddenly as he became interested in the child resting against the grandfather's side. "What's the little boy's name?" he asked.

"His name is actually Robert, but we call him Robin. What is yours?"

"Georgie. But I like Robin better."

"Yes, it's a nice name for a young child—and little Robin will always be young—"

"What makes you say that—don't he grow right?"

The grandfather ran his hand across the child's blond hair. His face was grave when he looked up at Georgie again. "No, Robin doesn't grow as he should. He's five years old and he can say only a few words—all the boys over at the school know that so I think I should tell you too. But we love Robin very much—when he and I meet any of the boys on our walks, they never fail to speak nicely to him—that pleases me very much."

Georgie put out his hand and touched Robin's foot gently. "Will he learn to read when he goes to school?" he asked.

"No."

"I can't either. I've been to school, but I ain't ever learned to read—"

The grandfather turned away from Robin and looked for a long time at his caller. "You've been hurt, Georgie. Were you in an accident?"

Here it was—the same old question that everybody asked of him and in a minute there would be more—maybe a lot more.

"No. I just got in a fight with some big kids."

"It must have been a very bad one." The grandfather, whose name was Hugh Collier, shook his head. "I've seen other children hurt the way you are, but their hurts didn't come from school-ground fights—grown-up people hurt those children—"

"Steve didn't hurt me—" Georgie said and then stopped quickly in sudden fright because he had mentioned that name.

Hugh Collier shook his head. "No, I suppose not." He looked at Georgie and there was a frown on his face.

Georgie felt uneasy. Finally he said, "You goin' to let me plant my bush here?"

"I'm sorry, Georgie but I have to say no. There are plenty of other places for your bush—"

"There ain't neither any other place," Georgie interrupted him in sudden fury. "You're a dumb old bastard and you don't know what you're talkin' about—" His voice broke, half sobbing and half screaming.

"All the same, Georgie, we have to face it—you must find another place for your bush. If we allow you to plant it here, other boys will want to come over and plant everything from sunflowers to cabbages—"

"I don't want to talk to you anymore—not to nobody." Georgie ran around the house back toward the school choking with his tears. Rosita came out on the back porch and Georgie heard her say, "What on earth—" but he didn't speak or look at her.

At five o'clock he didn't go in for supper and at six he once again did not go to vespers. Timothy found him at dusk, sitting on the street curb facing Mrs. Harper's garden.

Timothy was plainly out of patience with him. "Gosh, Georgie, don't you try to do the right things here at all? Sister Mary Angela was worried when you didn't come to supper—last night you didn't meet me where I told you to, and now tonight—" He broke off suddenly. "Where have you been, Georgie—just tell me that."

"I ain't been nowhere," Georgie muttered.

"You're actin' mean," Timothy said, but his voice was, for some reason, milder.

"I am mean. And I'm dumb. Leave me alone, will you?" Georgie glared at Timothy as he had glared at the gray-haired man across the street.

"Sure. Sure, I'll leave you alone." Timothy shrugged indifferently. "But then, lots of kids around here are mean and dumb. I am, myself, sometimes," he added and his words sounded proud.

Georgie closed his eyes for a few seconds. His head

ached worse than ever and the sore places across his back throbbed. He wanted to crawl into the cool bed where he slept the night before and lie in the dark where no one could see him. He knew that he couldn't, though. There were things he had to do before he could rest comfortably.

"Does your arm hurt you, Georgie?" Timothy asked after a while.

"No."

"How did it get hurt?"

"A big kid hit it when we had a fight." He looked at Timothy with dull eyes. "I thought Sister told you not to ask questions."

"Well, don't you want to go inside and get something to eat?" Timothy asked, refusing to be angered again.

"No, I just want to be by myself." He turned his back on Timothy. "Why don't you go away?" he asked wearily.

Timothy finally turned away and walked back toward the entrance of the building. Georgie leaned his head upon his knees and moaned softly in his anguish.

When he heard Sister Mary Angela say his name, he thought maybe she was going to scold him. But she didn't.

"Georgie, you must have something to eat before bedtime; you've hardly touched food all day. I know you feel strange and lonely right now, but you'll feel better soon. Come on; we'll get a glass of milk and some bread and butter from Sister Therese in the kitchen."

"No, I don't want nothin' to eat."

"Well, then, we'll get you ready for bed and I'll leave something on your bedside table. Maybe you'll feel like eating later on." She put her hand lightly on his head and ran her fingers through his hair, flinching as Georgie did, when she suddenly encountered a swollen knot hidden in the thick brown tangle just below his crown.

He got to his feet slowly, picking up the bush he had laid beside him. They put it back under his window and walked together into the building and down the long corridor to his room. He allowed her to help him off with his shirt, then he stood stolidly against the wall, trying to hide the wounds on his back.

"Nobody can look at my back 'cept in a hospital," he told her grimly. "Go away. I can get ready for bed by myself."

The world was black outside his window by the time he was in bed. He lay awake, wide-eyed and frightened at what he knew he must do, but determined and unyielding. When Sister Mary Angela looked in on him as she made her nightly rounds, he closed his eyes and lay unmoving on the pillow. She called to him softly, but when he made no reply she walked away closing the door quietly behind her.

He waited for a long time until everything was quiet along the corridor, then he slid out of bed and stood at the window looking out at the house across the street. Many windows were lighted and Georgie leaned against his own sill waiting for the lights to go out and for the time to come when he could safely believe that everyone who might possibly be looking out at the garden was in bed and asleep.

Underneath his window the rosebush leaned crookedly against the wall, wondering perhaps why Georgie was so slow in giving it the bed it needed, in giving it a chance to grow the scarlet roses that the tag tied around it had promised. He hurt at the thought of his bush feeling neglected and unloved.

A jet roared across the sky and Georgie's eyes followed the blinking lights until they were finally lost in darkness. As he watched the plane grow dimmer in the distance he thought of the lady in the garden—what if some day she would fly away across the sky into a place so far away that no one would ever see or hear of her again, leaving her garden for Georgie to look after, leaving the little boy to be his friend, to play with him among the bright flowers and under the trees. He wished desperately that such a thing might happen.

Finally all the lights were out except for a tiny glow from one of the second-floor windows. Georgie moved cautiously around his bed and opened the door of his room with great care, making no sound. He had learned to move stealthily—for a very long time it had been necessary to make no sound if he were to avoid Steve's hearing him. It had been good training for the project he now had in mind.

He walked barefoot down the corridor, breaking into a run on tiptoe as he neared the front door. The locks were simple—a great iron key had to be turned and then a sliding bolt could be moved back easily if one got it in its proper groove. Once the bolt was pressed back, the heavy wooden door opened noiselessly as if doing its best to cooperate with Georgie, to help him with the thing he had to do.

He thought suddenly of the unlocked door at the entrance to the apartment in Tampa, and the memory, together with the blackness of the night into which he stepped, sent a spasm of fear through his body.

He trembled as he thought of Steve stepping out of the shadows, grabbing him and throwing him to the ground. He stumbled at the thought and fell on the steps where he lay for a while gasping with fear. Then, finally, reassured by the silence around him, he crept around the building until he found the rosebush underneath his window.

"I didn't forget you—I didn't, I didn't," he repeated the words in a whisper over and over again as he tugged at the bush with his free hand. Then, pulling it beside him, he crossed the street and opened the gate that led into the garden. The latch clicked as the gate swung back into place, and Georgie cowered for a while, waiting to see if anyone had heard.

He needed a spade badly but there was none to be had and so with his hand he dug into the damp, sandy soil until he made a hole which he hoped was deep enough to take care of the long roots that must be covered. He did not know where to find water, but that was a matter for tomorrow and for the time being he pushed all tomorrows out of his mind. Tonight there was only one thing that really mattered: the rosebush was at last in the place that was right for it.

He stole back to the school's front door just as the bell in the tower chimed eleven times. Once inside, he turned the key carefully and slid the bolt in place as securely as Sister Mary Angela had done when she locked up for the night. Back in his room he noticed that the world rocked all about him; when he climbed into bed he clutched at the sides of his mattress for support until the beating of his heart quieted and he was able to sleep.

FIVE

"I saw her, Georgie. I don't know where she got it, but I saw her throw your rosebush down on the back playground—hard, like she was mad and hated it—" Timothy's eyes were wide as he stood in the doorway of Georgie's room.

Georgie froze beside his bed where he was trying with trembling hands to dress himself before the gong rang for breakfast. He stared back at Timothy, his eyes as wide as his friend's and much more frightened.

"She came up to Sister Dolores in the foyer and I heard her say she wanted to see Sister Mary Angela right away. And she wasn't kidding. She meant right away." He frowned, puzzled and plainly worried for Georgie. "Why do you suppose she'd want to be throwin' your bush around?" he asked.

"I planted it in her garden—last night," Georgie said wretchedly. He hurried past Timothy, pulling his shirt half over his shoulders as he ran down toward the door. Timothy, watching him, clasped one hand to his head partly in mock, partly in real horror.

Georgie found his forlorn bush lying on the playground and he gathered it to him as he had when the policeman rescued it from the janitor's trash barrels. The boys were all at breakfast by that time, and no one saw how tenderly he lifted his bush, holding it close to him.

In less than two minutes he was back at the garden fence, carrying the bush in his good arm, his thin face white with the sickness inside him and the anger.

He strode through the gate as if he were as tall as any man and walked down to the spot where a shallow hole in the sand marked the place he had given his rose the night before. When he approached it, he saw to his dismay that a dozen or more delicate lilies, just ready to bloom, had been broken or crushed by his feet the night before, that some of the bulbs were lying above ground and exposed to the hot sunlight. Remorsefully, he knelt and lifted plant after broken plant, trying to replace them in their bed, pressing sand firmly about them and digging holes in which he buried the bulbs that had been upturned.

He was still working when Molly Harper stepped up quietly beside him. Her voice was harsh when she called Georgie's attention to her presence. "I tore that bush out of the ground and threw it across the street a while ago," she told him, her blue eyes almost black with anger. "My husband planted calla lily bulbs for me here as a surprise because he knew I especially loved them. Every spring since then—" She broke off, and her voice grew more bitter than ever. "You ruined a dozen or more of them last night—you disobeyed both Sister and my father and came over here and ruined my lilies—"

Georgie was on his feet facing her, his bush close in his arms. "It was dark. I didn't mean to hurt them."

"Well, you did hurt them. And you came over here when you knew perfectly well that you had no right to be here—" She threw her braids back over her shoulders and Georgie thought they looked like yellow whips growing out of her head.

She took a step nearer to him. "Understand this, Georgie, once and for all, if I ever find that bush here again, I'll pull it up and throw it in the incinerator. Believe me, I mean that. Now get out of here this minute and don't ever let me see either you or your bush in this garden again."

At her words Georgie gave the shrill cry that had never failed to arouse Steve's rage. He glared at Molly like a furious little animal.

"If you ever do it—I . . . I'll set fire to your house—I'll kill you dead. I'll do the meanest things to you that ever happened—" His voice choked with dry sobs that shook his body.

He took a step toward her, his brown hands clenched tightly, his face intense and desperate. Then without warning, he crumpled and fell at her feet repeating something over and over. She had to lean down to hear his words. They were: "—have to plant it here—have to—have to plant it here—"

The left side of his shirt had been hung loosely over the cast on his arm; as he rolled from one side to the other, it fell off and Molly Harper had her first glimpse of an evil she hadn't guessed was there.

It was a purple and red mass of swollen flesh, welts and knots imposed one upon another, some of them beginning to heal, some oozing the yellowish liquid of infection. She stared in disbelief for several seconds, then she leaned down and touched the mutilated flesh.

"How did this happen, Georgie? Why were you hurt like this?" she asked hoarsely.

He sat up quickly and pushed her from him. "Don't you look at my back—nobody can see my back 'cept people in the hospital. Don't you ever dare look at my back again," he said, his sobs replaced by a hard coldness.

She stood looking down at him, her face now as white as his. "I'm not going to join the club of brutes, Georgie. Stay here with your bush—I have to find Sister Mary Angela—"

He hadn't understood her words. The storm inside him made words and garden, a strange, angry woman and even his rosebush seem dim and far away.

He lay in the sand, tired and hopeless. He didn't dare plant his bush again for the threat of the incinerator still rang in his ears; on the other hand, a fierce anger against the adults around him, who would not understand, hardened his determination to see that the rose remained in the garden where he knew it belonged.

It seemed that a long time passed while the sun grew hotter and more hurtful. His brain had shining wheels in it that turned faster and faster, making him dizzy and sick.

"Maybe we're goin' to die, both of us," he whispered to the bush beside him. He closed his eyes and did not know that Sister Mary Angela tried to waken him or that Mrs. Harper picked him up in her arms and carried him across the street to his room.

SIX

Georgie's fever ran high for five full days and during most of that time he tossed about in delirium, unaware of the need to protect the unhealed wounds on his back. With the resultant stinging which spread all over his back and buttocks, a picture of Steve materialized in his brain and filled him with terror. At such time Georgie's shrieks were terrible to hear, and Sister Mary Angela's face was drawn as she bent over him trying to soothe and comfort him.

At other times it was the safety of the rosebush that disturbed him. He saw it in his dreams, thrown like trash beside the calla lilies and scorned by proud flowers that turned into jeering boys. "Hello, Ugly," they whispered at first so that none of the Sisters could hear them. "Who beat the hell out of you, Ugly?" The voices then grew so loud at times that Georgie went wild with the din they set up in his brain, and as if she wanted to add to his distress, a woman with blazing eyes and long yellow whips of hair over her shoulders advanced toward the rosebush. What she intended to do with it was all too plain as she picked it up and dragged it away toward barrels filled with litter.

It was this vision of the woman that renewed the threats Georgie had made in the garden. "I'll burn your house; I'll kill you dead," he told the Molly Harper of his delirium while the real Molly Harper stood at Sister Mary Angela's side and tried to soothe him.

On the sixth day his fever subsided and he seemed much better until he recognized Molly bending over his bed. His eyes widened with fear at sight of her and he turned his back, shrinking as far away from her as possible.

Sister Mary Angela came to his bed after Molly left and sat beside him. "Mrs. Harper has been helping Dr. Blake and me take care of you, Georgie. She has been kind—"

He shuddered. "I hate her. She'll hurt my rose-bush again, I know she will. I'm so much afraid of her—"

"You've been sick for quite a long time, Georgie. I think the fever has made you have bad dreams—"

She said he'd been sick a long time. Anything could have happened in a long time. He looked at Sister Mary Angela with despair in his eyes. "You can tell me—she's throwed my bush away, ain't she? Like the janitor did that night in the apartment."

"If you will listen, Georgie, I'll tell you about your rosebush. Old Eddie made a bed for it over on this side of Mrs. Harper's garden—he put in the kind of food roses need and plenty of water. Your bush is standing over there waiting for you to get well and visit it. Nothing is going to hurt it—Mrs. Harper will never pull it up again."

The words were too good. They were like the words, "We'll never let Steve come here again—my boy won't have to be afraid anymore—" He suddenly hated Sister Mary Angela the way he hated his mother. "You are a old liar," he said angrily, "you are sayin' lies to me—" He pulled the sheet over his head and burrowed far down beneath it, crying and refusing either to listen or speak to her.

After a while when he was quieter she spoke to him again. "I've brought Timothy in to see you, Georgie; he wants to say hello."

Slowly he uncovered his head and looked up at his visitor. Timothy grinned uneasily at him.

"I got something to tell you, Georgie. All of us watched Old Eddie plant your rose—me and Sister and Robin's grandfather and Mrs. Harper—even fat ol' Coca-Cola Amanda brought little Robin down. We wanted to tell you about it, but you was too sick to listen—"

"You believe Timothy, don't you, Georgie?" Sister Mary Angela interrupted in a calm voice. "You don't believe that Timothy is an 'old liar,' do you?"

Georgie felt ashamed. "Nobody here is a old liar— Except her," he added stubbornly.

"She allowed your rosebush to be planted in her garden, Georgie—"

"The grandfather made her do it—I know he did— him and maybe the little boy—"

Timothy started to speak, but Sister Mary Angela shook her head at him. "We'll talk about it when Georgie is stronger, Tim. Let's do our chores now and let him sleep for a while—"

They walked away together and Georgie lay, uneasy

and wondering, but less agitated. Late that afternoon Sister Mary Angela let him sit up in a wheelchair and pushed him out on the side porch which faced the garden. "Look straight ahead, Georgie, down just beyond the gate. There's your bush standing up tall—looking better than it's ever looked since you brought it here—do you see it?"

He drew a long breath, half in relief, half in a fear that wouldn't quite leave him. "Will she hurt it some night when we're asleep?" he asked, hoping to be reassured.

"No one will hurt your bush. Absolutely no one. I give you my word. If I thought anyone were going to destroy it, I'd—I'd go out and do something about it. Can't you trust me?"

He nodded slowly. "Can't we go over and talk to it?"

"We must wait till you're stronger. I think in a few days you and I can walk over and have a visit with your friend."

"I think I'm well enough right now," he said, but he admitted to himself when he was back in his room that his bed felt good after being out of it for a while; that even the short trip to the porch had left a tiredness in him.

The tiredness was somehow good, though. He lay

in the clean white bed, relaxed and contented, glad to be alone and able to have a waking dream of what it would be like when he could be close to his bush again. After pain and a fear that had stayed with him constantly until it wore him out and made his body sick, after all the terrible days, his rosebush was safe and because of that it was safe for him to rest. Sister Mary Angela did not lie. He should have known she was not like his mother. She did not lie and he felt safe in believing that his rose was now where it belonged in the beautiful garden that was like a page in his flower book. It didn't matter that the garden belonged to her. The part of his brain that brought restful waking dreams to him pushed Mrs. Harper far away from his thoughts.

A few days later Sister Mary Angela took him across the building to a room she called the chapel. She wheeled him to a side door along one of the halls, and they were suddenly on a sort of balcony that she called the choir loft. Below them was a large room full of empty seats.

"That is where you will sit with the other boys when you come to vesper service," she said pointing down to the empty room. "Today I've brought you up here where we can talk for a while." She allowed him to get out of the wheelchair and sit beside her on a low bench near the organ. "I often come up here when I want to rest—or when I'm troubled—"

He looked up at her without answering. She, too, was quiet for a while, and then she said, "Do you know about God, Georgie?"

"No," he said, and added, "do you know about Him?"

"I often come up here to talk with Him."

"He's not in this room, is He?"

"He can hear us anywhere—if we really want to talk with Him."

"What do you talk about?" he asked, looking at her curiously.

"I ask Him sometimes to help me understand the world around me—" She paused as if she were thinking, as if she needed to find words. "The world is beautiful in so many ways, but it is very cruel too, in many other ways. There are such things as children being cold and hungry, being hurt by people with twisted minds. I get angry sometimes, and I ask Him to help me understand why these things should be—"

"The world is bad—all of it," he muttered. Then, remembering, he said, "All but my rosebush. It's good."

She was silent again for a while, then she asked, "If

you could ask God to do something for you, Georgie, what would it be?"

His answer came without hesitation. "Have a policeman kill Steve and Miss Cressman—and her," he said, anger coming back to his eyes.

Sister Mary Angela raised her eyes to the ceiling. "I think we are not yet attuned to Thy Presence," she said quietly.

Her voice was very low, but Georgie heard her. "What did them words mean?" he asked.

"In a way, I was just telling God that I'm sorry you can't forgive Mrs. Harper."

He did not reply at first, then he said, "She hurt my rosebush, she said mean things—you'd better tell Him that—"

She suddenly seemed to think they should talk about something else. "Do you like to listen to music, Georgie?"

"I ain't never listened," he answered.

She rose and went up to seat herself at the organ. "Well, I love music the way you love flowers. Sometimes I like to come up here and play the organ so that I can relax and forget the things that may be troubling me. You listen and see if you like my music."

Her hands touched the keys and they made a quiet

singing for a few minutes. Then she pushed some of the little squares in front of her and the singing swelled until it filled the whole chapel and echoed as if there was a great happiness inside the organ and it was telling everyone who listened that not quite all the world was bad.

Georgie caught his breath as the music grew louder and sweeter; when it finally turned to a whisper and then stopped altogether, he looked up at Sister Mary Angela with wonder. "How can you make it sound like that?" he asked.

"Because I've trained my fingers for many years," she answered, "and because I love music so much."

There was a catch in his voice as he spoke. "It's nice," he said.

She smiled at him. "Yes, I'm glad you liked it, Georgie."

As they prepared to go back to his room, Georgie turned to her again. "Can I come back and hear the music sometime?"

"Of course."

Georgie noticed that her eyes looked full of happiness about something.

The next day Timothy came up to Georgie's room and sat with him for an hour. Georgie was strained and uneasy with his caller at first, but no one stayed uneasy with Timothy for very long. Sister Mary Angela called him her "public relations" boy; Timothy had no idea what she meant by that, but he assumed from her tone that it was good.

"It was nice that Mrs. Harper let your rosebush be planted in her garden, wasn't it, Georgie?" he asked.

Georgie's dark eyes glinted. "The little boy's grandfather made her do it," he said grimly. Then honesty made him add, "Anyway, I think that's what happened."

Timothy was thoughtful for a minute. "She used to be friendlier—that was before Paul and his dad got killed. She used to say hi to us once in a while, and once she had a birthday party for Paul—all of us that was about his age got to go—"

"Did you ever go over there just to play with—the boy?" For some reason Georgie did not wish to say Paul.

"Sure—a few times. Paul invited me to go swimming with him in the lake one time—me and Kevin, I think it was. And one other time I went with Paul when he took Robin down to feed the duck family on the lake." Timothy laughed at something he remembered. "That was a big deal for Robin. He'd hold tight to Paul's hand and yell and try to jump up and down when he saw the ducks fightin' over the bread we threw to them—"

Georgie smiled. "He's a nice little kid, I guess."

"Yeah." Timothy pulled at his ear and frowned. "Yeah, he's all right, but you have to be awful patient with a kid like Robin. He wouldn't be still five minutes when me and Paul wanted to sit in the playhouse their grandfather made for them in the banyan tree. We wanted to talk a while and make plans for buildin' a birdhouse. But Robin kept buggin' us to take him back to the lake so he could see the ducks—"

"Did you ever build the birdhouse?" Georgie asked.

Timothy shook his head. "The week after I was there, Paul got killed—"

The memory seemed to make Timothy sad. He rose to leave shortly afterward.

"Sister said I mustn't wear you out." He extended his hand for the handshake he had been taught to make upon leaving. Georgie had shaken hands only a few times before—never with another child. He was shy and somewhat embarrassed, but pleased too. He liked Timothy.

By the next day he was beginning to fret at not being able to go over to the garden. "I feel so good,

Sister. Why can't I go over and see my rosebush?" he asked as soon as she came in to see him.

"The doctor thinks that you can go out for a while tomorrow. Let's rest now and be ready to go over in the morning."

"Before breakfast?"

"Afterward. Then you can stay longer."

"You won't forget you promised?"

She sighed. "Georgie, I make promises to dozens of boys every week—almost every day. I never yet have forgotten one of them. I promise you again—you'll see your rosebush tomorrow."

SEVEN

Georgie had two other visitors just before supper-time that evening. He had not seen Robin's grand-father since their first meeting that day on the porch. Now, suddenly, he appeared at the door of Georgie's room, one hand full of thin, brightly colored books, the other leading Robin.

"Sister Mary Angela said that you might like to hear a story before you have your supper," he said, laying the books down and shaking Georgie's hand as politely as Timothy had done. "Robin wanted to come along—is that all right with you?"

"Yes, I like Robin." Georgie did not often look

pleased, but he smiled at the little boy who looked up at him with wide eyes.

"How about stories—do you like them too?"

Georgie shrugged and his face turned sullen. "I don't know any, 'cause I don't know how to read."

"Well, I'll do the reading while you and Robin listen. I love to read to children—I used to read to Robin's brother, Paul, every night when he was little—"

Georgie did not answer. Mr. Collier lifted Robin up beside Georgie where he sat propped up by the pillows placed at his back. The two boys looked up silently, one face glowering, the other seeming to be concerned with something far away.

Mr. Collier looked through the books he had brought with him and finally selected one about a boy who was in many ways something like Georgie. It was the story of a lonely boy who was treated cruelly by grown-up people—a boy who loved singing but who could sing only when he was alone, when the moon and the woods made the time and place right for his singing. There was suffering in the story, words that brought tears to Georgie's eyes and had to be brushed quickly away before anyone saw them, but at last everything was right because one good person understood the boy and became his friend.

As he read, Mr. Collier sat on the bed beside the children and kept the book before them so that they could follow the story with the bright pictures on each page. Georgie sat quietly, listening to every word; once without thinking of what he was doing, he laid his right arm around Robin's shoulders. He noticed that Mr. Collier's voice shook a little at that moment, but very quickly became deep and strong again.

When the story was finished, the grandfather closed the book and stretched his arms out toward Robin. "We must be going now, Georgie. Rosita will scold me if I keep Robin out beyond his suppertime." He stopped at the door and turned to face Georgie again. "By the way, we gave your rosebush a drink of water as we came over. Old Eddie walked down to the gate with us and he said to tell you that your bush looks healthy—he thinks it's going to grow well."

"I'm goin' to see it tomorrow," Georgie told him. "Sister promised me that I could."

"Good. I think it will be glad—no, not just glad—I think it will be very happy to see you. I've read somewhere that roses are particularly sensitive flowers—"

"What's 'sensitive'?"

"A sensitive person—or flower—understands how other people feel. They're sad when someone else is sad, happy when someone else is happy. If that is true, your rosebush will understand how happy you are tomorrow—"

"Sensitive," Georgie whispered the word himself. "A rose is sensitive." He liked the new word.

Mr. Collier loosed his hold on the pile of books he held and one of them slid to the floor. Georgie noticed that it was the one about the lonely boy who loved to sing. He put out his hand and pointed toward it. "Can I keep that one? I'll be careful." All at once he was terribly eager to hold and look at this book.

"Of course, Georgie. Do you want to look at the pictures?"

"I might try to read it," Georgie answered. "I might learn myself to read it out loud to Robin and my rosebush." He took the book from Mr. Collier's hand. "Look, I learned some of the words while you was reading—" He ran his fingers along a line. "The boy was standing in the moonlight woods—" he read, and looked up at Mr. Collier proudly.

The man looked at the line Georgie read—only one word was wrong. The sentence read: "The boy was standing in the moonlit woods."

"I know some of it already, don't I?" Georgie asked eagerly.

"Yes, you do, Georgie," Mr. Collier said slowly. "I wonder—maybe you are ready to read and no one has ever realized it. Maybe you wanted to read this story because you liked it better than the ones in your schoolbooks—"

"Books in school are crap," Georgie answered shortly, "and long rows of words you have to say without a story—they're crap too. This one is a good story."

"I'm glad you liked it. This book used to belong to my grandson. He would be about your age if he were living. The book is precious to his mother, but I know she'll be happy for you to keep it for a while—"

Georgie's face changed quickly. "I don't want it if it's hers," he said, closing the book and extending it coldly toward the old man.

Mr. Collier looked distressed. "My daughter would want you to keep the book for as long as you need it, Georgie. She would know that, of course, you'd take good care of it—"

"I don't want her book. I don't like her, and I don't want anything that's hers—"

"Except a place in her garden for your rosebush," the grandfather reminded him gently.

Georgie brushed those words aside. "That don't

count," he said evenly. "That garden was the right place. No matter who said she owned it—"

Mr. Collier smoothed his beard for a minute, then he laid the books down and lifted Robin back on the bed.

"You told me a while ago that you couldn't read, Georgie."

"I can't," Georgie barked out the words, forgetting how proud he had been in recognizing a sentence just a short time before.

"But you recognized several words just now, didn't you? I think I might be able to teach you to read if we both tried hard."

"Nobody couldn't teach me to read. I'm dumb."

"I don't believe that. I think you may be a very bright boy who has never had people around him who cared whether he could read or not."

Georgie was silent. He was thinking of Miss Cressman, of his mother and Steve.

Mr. Collier took a paper from his pocket and smoothed out the blank side of it. "Here—I'm going to start a story about your rosebush," he said and hurriedly wrote a couple sentences. "I'll make it tell the reader who is talking—'I am a rosebush who lives in a beautiful Florida garden'—and here it says that it belongs to a boy named Georgie, who loves flowers more than anything in the world. Now, would you like to add to the story? I'll do the printing for you."

The sullen look disappeared from Georgie's face as he sat up straighter. "Say that one time it lived in a grocery store, say that the numbers that winned it to me went like this: 8662 dash 71 dash 4923. Say that it is sensitive—Say that a man named Old Eddie planted it for me when I was sick and give it fertilizer and stuff to make it grow—"

"That's a good story," Mr. Collier said when Georgie hesitated. "And shall I write the names of all the people who are trying to help the rosebush grow healthy and be able to bloom? Here is Georgie, first of all; next is Sister Mary Angela; here are Old Eddie and Rosita and Amanda, here are Robin and his mother, and here I come next, the grandfather winding up the list."

He placed the paper in Georgie's hand and read it aloud, his finger moving along each line. Georgie's eyes shone with interest as he listened, then he pushed Mr. Collier's hand aside and read the paragraph himself with very little help. However, when he came to the words "Robin's mother" he stopped short and reached for Mr. Collier's pencil. "We don't need her in the story," he said, drawing a line through the words and then resuming a pleased inspection of the paragraph.

"Put lots of these words in another story and see if I know them," he ordered, and when Mr. Collier had written another paragraph using many of the same phrases, Georgie read it with an ease that amazed both reader and teacher. "I'm reading, ain't I?" he asked, and Mr. Collier nodded thoughtfully.

"We'll find stories that you enjoy hearing, Georgie. I'll read many, many stories to you—maybe I can write some for you if you will help me by suggesting things you'd like to put in them. Do you think we might work together?"

"Yes. We'll write some easy stories at first—so Robin and my rosebush can understand them when I read out loud."

When Mr. Collier left with Robin, going down the corridor toward Sister Mary Angela's office, Georgie rolled his head on the pillow enjoying the unexpected pleasure of the moment. He felt so much better that he got out of bed and sat in the chair beside his window.

Outside the sky flamed as the sun set and across the street the garden lay like a bright picture. The colors glowed with a special light, giving their best before twilight robbed them of their brightness. Georgie believed that he could see the outlines of his bush down beside the big gate.

"I can read," he whispered, full of wonder at the thought. "I can read rosebush and sensitive and fertilizer and Robin just as good as anyone. I can read them in one story and then in another one. It wasn't just remembering where a word was—it was real reading."

He was examining the paper Mr. Collier had left with him when Sister Mary Angela came in with his supper tray. "Sister, I can read," he told her.

"I've heard about it, Georgie, and I'm very happy. Mr. Collier thinks that you've learned a lot in your classroom, but that something kept you from showing your teacher how much you knew. Do you think he may be right?"

"Ever'thing was mean," he answered, immediately subdued.

"I know." She set his supper on the bedside table without speaking further.

She sat quietly watching him as he ate. She thought of the words "mentally challenged" on his record from the Tampa school. There were more words: inattentive, destructive, filthy, incorrigible—She studied his face and wondered what words might have been on his record if he had not been half-starved all his life, if he had never known what it was like to be beaten regularly and to live in constant terror. Her face became grim at her thoughts.

She was quiet for so long that Georgie began watching her closely. "Are you mad, Sister?" he asked after a while.

She managed a quick smile. "Not at you, Georgie." Her face changed then and she leaned forward, seeming to forget whatever it was that had been bothering her.

"We are very fortunate to have Mr. Collier here to help you, Georgie. He once taught young men and women in college how to be good teachers—especially how to teach children who had lived, as you said just now, where 'everything was mean.' He even went into the poorer sections of big cities and found out in many cases what things were preventing children from learning. So you see, he knows a great deal about helping you to read."

"Yes," Georgie agreed, "he wants me to help him write the kind of stories that I like. And he's going to look for a lot of already wrote ones—"

She nodded. "That's right. He told me a little about his plan when he came down to my office. He thinks you and he should work together from now on and that you shouldn't start class with the other boys until after the summer vacation—" She paused, looking at Georgie thoughtfully. "Maybe by that time Judge O'Neill will find someone who will see to it that you are able to stay here—"

Georgie hardly noticed what she said. He was thinking: "Maybe Robin's grandfather can learn me to read before I had to go to school—maybe the other kids won't know that I was dumb at first—"

She rose and laid a hand on the cast that protected his arm. "I must go to chapel now. I'll leave your door open so that you can hear the music. Would you like that?"

"Yes," he said. "You play the organ real good, Sister."

He ate his supper slowly and when the tinkling bell sounded throughout the building announcing that it was time for music and prayers in the chapel, he got up from his chair and went to sit outside his room, placing a pillow between the doorjamb and his tender back.

The school was cool and quiet in the twilight, all the noise of a houseful of boys silenced because every boy except Georgie was in the chapel. He liked the stillness with only the sound of music flowing around him while pictures of his new life came to his mind, one after another.

He thought of the story in the book with all the bright pictures and the wonder of his recognizing a sentence in it; he thought of his rosebush, well and happy, looking forward to his visit in the morning. He thought of Robin leaning against his side while the grandfather read to them, and he smiled to himself. Things were not all mean any longer. Just Mrs. Harper. Just her.

When the service in the chapel was over the boys could be heard rushing outside for another hour of play before bedtime, congregating in the front parlor to read or play checkers or chess, standing around in little groups laughing and talking.

Georgie was pleased to see Timothy appear at his door when the play hour was almost over.

"Have you heard about the present Judge O'Neill sent out for us this evening?" Timothy asked.

"No." Georgie remembered the judge well. Big eyebrows—he liked roses—he was going to find some rich man who would pay Sister Mary Angela so that Georgie could live at the school.

"Air mattresses," Timothy explained hurriedly and

seated himself on the foot of Georgie's bed. "He sent ten of them and Sister Monica is goin' to let the guys at my end of the corridor have the first sleep-out on them 'cause we're the youngest—"

Georgie felt envious, but he didn't have anything to say. Timothy looked at him anxiously, "I know you're still not too well, Georgie, but you're my friend and so I thought I'd ask you anyway: would you like to sleep outside on one of the air mattresses tonight?"

It was the first time Georgie could remember that another child had invited him to share something that promised to be fun.

"I'd like to," he said. "Do you suppose Sister will let me?"

"I've been twistin' her arm. She'll be here before long—we'll see what she says."

Sister Mary Angela came to the room only a few moments later. Timothy met her at the door. "He wants to, Sister. He says he'd like to sleep outside with us."

"You know Georgie has been very sick, Timothy?"

"Yes, ma'am. But I think it will help him to get well quicker if he can be outside with us."

She turned to look at Georgie. "I really don't see why he shouldn't—there'll be no roughhousing out there, Tim?"

"No way," Timothy assured her. "Sister Monica says we have to pipe down early so the rest of you can sleep. We're just goin' to talk a little, maybe tell some jokes and make up some lies. We won't be horsin' around—"

When Timothy raced back down the corridor to tell the others that Georgie could join them, Sister Mary Angela shook a small white pill from the bottle on Georgie's dresser. "I think I'll give you some of the medicine Doctor Blake left so that you'll be sure to get to sleep. You need plenty of rest while your body is getting strong again."

She walked down to the back lawn with him and watched as Sister Monica handed out mattresses and sheets, giving orders as to where they should be placed—"A big circle to make conversation easier," she explained to Sister Mary Angela. "And hopefully a little quieter," she added laughingly.

Among the ten boys sprawling on their mattresses, nine laughed and bragged and jeered at one another while the tenth one of them quietly listened. Georgie had no jokes to tell; he had lied often, but his lies were not funny, made-up ones that Timothy and his friends told. "Once when I was a cattle-rustler out in Colorado—" That was a lie very different from the one which claimed that Georgie had not set fire to a pile of papers under Miss Cressman's car.

To listen to the others was fun, though. Sometimes he laughed a low laugh that no one heard; after an especially funny joke he would think: "Tomorrow I'll tell that to my rosebush."

"These mattresses are O.K., ain't they?" a dark boy named Terry asked. "The old judge had a bright idea this time."

"This time, yes. Last time, no!" Timothy interrupted. "Remember last fall when he sent cartons of bath soap and powder for athlete's foot? Wow!"

"That wasn't the judge's present. That come from one of his rich friends—"

"Whoever it was—wow!"

"Oh, well, you win a few and you lose a few," a boy they called Kevin said mildly.

"I got invited to go to town in the station wagon and help Sister Monica pick these mattresses up at the post office," Terry said, looking pleased with himself.

"What's so super about goin' into town in the station wagon?" Timothy asked scornfully. "Nuts to you, Terry."

Terry shrugged. "Oh, well, it was fun. We drove

back on the lake road 'cause Sister wanted to see what birds are out on the lake so far this spring. We saw two blue heron, and an egret—there's about a thousand gulls out there and there's a new family of ducks quackin' and swimmin' around in circles like a bunch of dumbskies—"

"Maybe that's the reason Robin likes them so much—dumbskies like other dumbskies—" a dark-haired boy giggled.

"Shut your big mouth, Richie," several of the boys yelled together.

"Yeah, Richie, shut up—" the voice was Timothy's. "That's a cheap shot, makin' fun of Robin."

"Paul would hate you for that, Richie," another boy scolded. Then he turned to Timothy. "Does Georgie know about Paul?"

"Yes, I told him," Timothy answered.

The voices had been growing loud during the past few minutes and now Sister Monica appeared on the balcony above the night campers.

"It's a quarter to ten, gentlemen. Get those voices down and either be asleep or act like you're asleep by ten o'clock. Otherwise—whoosh! You and your mattresses will be sucked up by a strong wind and landed in your rooms upstairs—"

Georgie sank back into his mattress, glad of the cool, fragrant air that surrounded him. The pills were already making him drowsy; it was pleasant to feel sleep overcoming him as he listened to whispers and low giggles around him. He was the first boy among the ten to get to sleep within Sister Monica's fifteen-minute order.

It was still dark when he awoke, refreshed and ready to begin an important day. When he heard the bell in the front tower chime four times he thought he couldn't live through the long line of hours that must pass before he would walk across the street and into the garden for his promised visit with the rosebush.

He was wide awake and tired of any bed after many days of illness and inactivity. He sat up and looked across the street where darkness covered everything, allowing only gray outlines of the big white house to show through the night and the blacker shadows of tall palms on the school ground to shift lazily in the breeze. He could barely recognize Timothy sound asleep on the mattress beside him; the dim figures of the other boys sprawled a short distance away.

He breathed deeply of the fragrant air that drifted across from the garden, feeling almost giddy with the heavy perfume and the softness of the night air. Above him the sky had stars scattered all over it, some so low that a boy able to climb the highest palm with an arm suddenly well again, might pull some of them down and watch the light flash in them as they were dropped from one hand to the other.

He dreamed of that possibility for a while and the earliness of the hour together with the darkness pushed the real world away from him. He seemed to hear voices all around him. "How did you ever get them out of the sky?" the voices wondered. "What are you going to do with them stars, Georgie?"

After a while he heard Timothy, excited and pleading: "Can I hold one of them, Georgie, just for a little while?"

His own voice had grown deep and quiet like Mr. Collier's when he answered: "No Timothy, you can't. They belong to Mrs. Harper's boy—the one that would be as old as us if he wasn't dead—"

After a while another voice called him. It was faint and far away, but it insisted that he listen. "Why do you have to wait all those hours till tomorrow, Georgie? I need to talk to you—right now."

He rose quietly from his mattress and stood listening intently. After a minute he walked very slowly across the wide lawn and into the street. "Of course," he thought, "of course I have to do it."

Out in the street he stood with his good arm outstretched, his face turned up to the starry sky. He laughed softly to himself as the light wind ran through his hair.

"I am like the boy in the story—I am all alone in the night and nobody can see me." He wished that he could sing as the boy in the story sang, but he didn't know a single song although that evening his throat had tightened as if it had wanted very much to sing when he heard Sister Mary Angela's music coming from the chapel.

"But anyway, I have a rosebush!" That was enough. He knew that the cuts and scars and purple spots made his face ugly, he knew that he couldn't sing, that he couldn't read the way Mrs. Harper's boy had probably been able to read. His joy, however, was above all that. He had his rosebush and in another minute it would know he had not forgotten it, that at four o'clock in the morning he was not afraid to come to the garden and visit with his friend.

The thought sent him hurrying down the street. He tried to run, but his legs were still like rubber and he was forced to move slowly, glad to grasp the wickets of the garden fence occasionally and wait for his legs to relearn something they had forgotten while he lay in bed.

When he reached the rosebush at last, he found it tall and still a little frail-looking, but beautiful in his eyes. He sat down near its base and grasped the cluster of stems closest to the ground.

"Do you want to know something about me?" he asked eagerly. "I can read!"

He waited just a second and then he felt the rose-bush tremble with joy and surprise. Georgie hugged it, remembering what the grandfather had said about roses being sensitive. "You are, too," he said. "You understand, and you know what, I'm not even dumb anymore. I'm even smart enough to read in a book that belonged to her boy—if I wanted to. But I don't. I won't read any of her books. She pulled you up and said she'd throw you in the incinerator. She would, too, except that Sister and Robin's grandfather won't let her. I hate her. I'll always hate anybody that is mean to you—"

Up in the big house he noticed the one window where a dim light showed. "The grandfather prob-ably leaves a light so the little boy won't be afraid," he thought. "I'll read to him as soon as I learn more." He turned again to the rosebush. "And I'll come here and read stories to you, too. You'll like my stories, I know you will. You're my friend, my sensitive rosebush." The word felt good on Georgie's tongue.

He bent his knees and lowered his head upon them, pleased that stretching the muscles of his back did not hurt as much as it had before he was sick. Keeping his good arm around the bush, he let his head rest against his knees and sat very still while drowsiness returned and pulled at his eyelids. A scampering lizard ran over his bare toes and a sudden flutter in a nearby cluster of flowers suggested that a snake might be out foraging for an early breakfast. Some insect took a vicious bite at one of his ankles, and a night bird hidden in one of the trees complained that Georgie had no business to be in the garden at a little after four in the morning.

"I'll tell on you," it rasped over and over in such strident tones that a whispering and then a chattering commenced all through the garden, as dozens of birds woke up early.

Over at the school the big bell in the tower chimed once which meant it was now half-past four. Georgie's head grew heavier on his knee until the knee collapsed, letting him tumble to the ground. He pressed his face close to the base of the rosebush and muttered, "Just a minute—just another minute and I'll go back—"

Then his body relaxed in the soft sand and he slept deeply, unworried and unafraid—

EIGHT

Sometimes when the birds talked loudly in the early morning they wakened Robin. Not Amanda. Amanda liked to sleep even when the sun came in at Robin's window and it was plainly time to get out of bed and to be carried downstairs. Lazy Amanda. That's what Rosita said.

Robin looked at the little lamp still glowing on his dresser. Mother pointed to the lamp many times. Your brother gave it to you, Robin. The lamp is a glass puppy begging for something to eat. Your big brother gave you the lamp that is like a puppy for your birthday.

Brother meant Paul. Robin could not say Paul, but he could hear the name somewhere inside him. Paul was fun. Sometimes Paul and Robin would fall on the ground and roll over and over. Once Paul played a game with Daddy and a big ball. They laughed when they said things together. Robin wanted to laugh too. Daddy said yes, Robin, of course you can laugh with us. You can laugh and play a game with Daddy and your big brother. Robin couldn't catch the ball, but that didn't matter. Paul pulled Robin to the ground and they rolled over and over and laughed a lot—both of them.

Sometimes Robin took a walk in the garden with Paul. Sometimes they stopped to look at a funny hoppy-toad. Ask him where he's going, Robin. Try, Robin. Try to say where are you going, hoppy-toad? Always Paul would say try, Robin. Try to say what I tell you. Robin tried to say the words Paul wanted him to say but he couldn't.

Ducks. Robin loved the ducks that went fast, fast in the water, going around and splashing water with their funny feet. Silly ducks. Paul called them silly ducks. They swim round and round and don't know where they're going. But we'll go down and feed them anyway, Robin. We'll feed the silly ducks. Rosita will give us some bread. Rosita would say, be careful, Paul. Keep Robin's hand in yours, Paul. Then they would go to feed the ducks and Robin would be happy.

Be careful, Paul. Mother would say the same words Rosita said. Daddy would say them too. And Grandfather. Be careful of your little brother, Paul. Never leave him alone for a minute. Always be careful.

Paul got mad sometimes. I'm always careful of my little brother. Do you have to tell me every time? Yes, every time until you're never able to forget. Did you lock the big gate, Paul? Did you be careful to get the iron hoop over the gate post? Yes, yes, I was careful. You know I'm careful, don't you, Robin?

They took the bread Rosita gave them down to the lake. Break it in little pieces, Robin. Now we will wade into the water. Only a little way that can't hurt us. Hold my hand, Robin, so you won't fall. Now give me a piece of bread.

Paul was big and strong. He could throw the bread far out on the water. Come on, silly ducks. Come and get the breakfast Robin has brought for you. You don't have good manners, do you, ducks? You grab your breakfast and bite one another. Robin has good manners. He doesn't grab and he tries hard to say please. You don't even try. Paul scolded the ducks like that, but he liked them. So did Robin. It was so much fun to feed the ducks with Paul.

Paul found a place to sit under the big tree close to the lake. This is our little house, Robin. You must sit here beside me and I will read a story to you. But to sit for a long time was bad. One day Robin got tired of hearing Paul say words out of the book. He tore some of the pages in the book. He scratched Paul's face and made red marks on it. Daddy said don't do that again, Robin. Your brother was trying to be good to you. But saying a story was not good. Not fun like feeding the ducks.

Paul went away in the car with Daddy one day. Robin cried because he wanted to go too. We have to hurry, Robin, Daddy said. You stay and take care of Mother. Paul said we'll be back in time for supper, Robin. After that we'll start making a house for the pretty birds. You can help me, Robin.

Robin liked to help Paul. He waited and waited for Paul to come back with Daddy. He had to go to bed when it was dark. When the birds woke him in the morning he waited and waited again. For a long time he waited to help Paul make a house for the birds in the garden.

When Grandfather carried him downstairs and

put him on the floor Robin looked in all the corners to see if Paul was playing the hiding game he played sometimes. Robin couldn't walk fast when he wasn't holding to Paul's hand. But he could walk a little. He walked slowly to every room and then he went out to Rosita's kitchen. He tried to say Paul to her and Rosita knew what he was trying to say. She held him too tight and cried and cried. Robin wanted down. He wanted to go on looking for Paul. But he never did find him.

Robin stopped trying to say words. Paul wasn't there to say try, Robin, try to say the words I tell you. And no one ever took him down to feed the ducks after Paul went away in the car with Daddy. There wasn't any fun with Paul gone. Mother was good and Grandfather and Rosita and Old Eddie. When Amanda came to live with them she was good too. But not fun. Big people were not fun. Robin needed Paul to play with him. But it was a long time that Paul didn't come back to build a house for the birds. Robin almost forgot about fun because Paul stayed away so long.

Once when he sat on Grandfather's lap a boy came up to the door. The boy was big like Paul but his face was hurt and it looked mad. His face wasn't like Paul's.

Yesterday Robin went with Grandfather to the big house where lots of boys live. Grandfather took books and they walked and walked until they found the boy. I will read a story to you Grandfather said. Robin didn't like stories out of a book, but he liked to look at nice colors in the pictures. The boy pointed to the pictures for Robin. Once he smiled at him. Once the boy put his arm around Robin's shoulder.

The light in the windows was getting brighter and brighter. Amanda was still asleep. Lazy Amanda would sleep all day if Rosita or Mother didn't call her.

Robin pulled himself to the edge of his crib which stood against the wall. That side of the crib was down and if he pushed against the wall he could move the crib away from it. Away and a little more away and finally far enough so that he could slide out of the open side and get down to the floor. That made him proud. Robin big boy, he thought. Paul would say Robin, you found a way to get out of the crib by yourself. You're a big boy.

He tottered across the room to a long window where the sill was low enough for him to see across it. Placing his hands on the cool marble sill he looked out at the garden where butterflies and ants and hoppy-toads were waiting for him to come out and play with them.

Suddenly away down at the edge of the garden

he saw a boy. It wasn't Paul. Almost though. Almost another Paul. There was a lady there and she was helping the boy stand up because the boy was tottery like Robin. When he could finally stand by himself, she took the boy's hand and they walked away. They didn't look up at Robin's window. They just went away toward the big house.

Robin wanted to cry. He wanted the boy that was like Paul to come to him. He wanted the boy to make a house for the birds and to let Robin help him. All at once he thought how much fun it would be to walk down to the lake on a morning like this.

"Come here, boy," something inside him cried while he beat his hands against the window. "Come and take a walk with Robin." He wanted to say the words. Paul would say, try hard, Robin. Try to say the words.

Robin tried hard. He tried to do what Paul told him to do. And all at once, he could. All at once Robin could say, "Feed ducks. Feed ducks."

NINE

After many weeks the boy that looked back at Georgie from his mirror was as changed as the rest of his life had changed. His arm was healed and well again, the heavy cast thrown away. The bruises and discolorations had faded and his cheeks had taken on the rosiness of Timothy's—but without Timothy's freckles. His thick brown hair was shining after the regular shampoos that Sister Monica insisted that he take, and it had been allowed to grow until it covered the crumpled ear and a part of the white streak extending down his neck.

"I think we have a fine-looking young man here,

Sister." The barber who came out once a month to the school turned Georgie's head this way and that, swirling some of the brown curls across his forehead, snipping a bit more above the collar.

Sister Dolores, who was supervising the haircuts that month, turned Georgie around to inspect him. "A new haircut and studying with Mr. Collier have made a new boy out of this one," she told the barber. Then she gave Georgie a light smack and told him to run along to his lessons.

He and the grandfather had worked together during the weeks of early spring and summer. At first Mr. Collier came over to the school and read many books to Georgie in his room; later he took his pupil down to the banyan-tree playhouse and there they wrote stories together which Georgie read aloud and then listened happily as the grandfather praised him.

One day they taped Georgie's reading on the little recorder Mr. Collier brought over to the school. Georgie was fascinated by the sound of his own voice reading through a long paragraph which would have been a puzzle to him a few months earlier. They continued the taping from time to time and as the days passed, Mr. Collier would replay the first tapes, allowing Georgie to hear and estimate his progress.

By mid-summer Georgie was able to read simple stories and he was happy to read aloud to anyone who would listen. He read to his rosebush, to Mr. Collier, to some of the nuns who were his special friends. All of them, even the rosebush, told him that he was reading so well that they felt very proud of him.

Sometimes Sister Mary Angela would invite him to come into her office and read to her while she leaned far back in the swivel chair in front of her desk and closed her eyes so that she could listen better. Then, when he was finished with his story, they would often talk together about other stories he had read, about baseball and arithmetic and caring for flowers—especially roses.

"Do you like living here at this school, Georgie?" she asked him one day.

She asked the question so suddenly that he was surprised. He had just lived there and learned his way around and things were nice, but he hadn't thought about liking to live there. Then when he thought about Sister's question he realized that, yes, he liked it very much. He liked learning to read, and feeling safe at night, and having friends like Timothy and little Robin. He nodded to Sister Mary Angela. "Yes, ma'am, I like it here," he told her.

"Then I guess you want to stay, don't you?" she asked.

Georgie was puzzled. "Do you mean maybe I can't stay?" he asked.

Sister Mary Angela smiled at him. "No, I don't mean that. You can stay, and I'm happy about that. We were troubled for a while about finding the money it takes to keep you here, but now everything is settled—"

"Does it cost a lot to be here?" He was worried.

Sister Mary Angela leaned over and took his hand. "Yes, a place like this costs a good deal of money, Georgie, but someone came in yesterday and gave me a check which will pay all of your expenses for a year. Do you know who it was?"

He shook his head and she smiled at the relief in his face. "It was Mrs. Harper," she said quietly.

He looked down at the floor without speaking.

"Can you forgive her now, Georgie?"

After a long time he muttered, "I hate people that hurt my bush—"

"But she changed her mind, Georgie; she allowed you to put your bush in her garden—"

He shook his head. "Robin's grandfather and you made her do it—She don't dare be mean to it while you're watching—"

Sister Mary Angela sat unmoving for a while; when she spoke her voice was very firm. "When I lived in the north a few years ago, Georgie, my car used to get stuck in ruts on the country roads I had to travel. The ruts were deep and packed with snow that melted and turned into ice. You should have seen the tires spin in those icy ruts when I tried to get my car out on level ground again—they'd whirl round and round, getting absolutely nowhere except maybe a little deeper in the ice—" she paused and looked directly into his eyes. "That's the way your anger toward Mrs. Harper behaves, Georgie; it spins round and round and gets nowhere—just deeper and more hurtful to all of us who want to see you out on level ground—"

He waited a long time before he replied. Then he said quietly, "I can't help it, Sister."

She just looked at him. "Then we'll have to wait until the ice melts—" She seemed to be talking to herself.

Georgie was able to look above or beyond—sometimes it seemed even through Molly Harper without so much as blinking or changing his expression. With Robin, however, his tenderness was as warm as his dislike for Robin's mother was icy. Timothy noticed all this and took his friend to task. "I know she was mean about the rosebush, but after all, you had smashed her calla lilies. If she was nice enough to let Old Eddie plant your bush over there, I think you might unbend her way a little—"

After that speech Timothy was avoided for days while Georgie gave all of his attention to Robin and the rosebush.

Robin would go with his grandfather down to the banyan-tree playhouse and sit, protesting and wiggling, while Mr. Collier read aloud to Georgie, waiting for the minute the book was closed and signs were made that the lesson was ended. Then he would run to Georgie's side, babbling excitedly, pulling and tugging at his arms to gain attention. They would romp together then, rolling in the grass, digging in the white sand along the lakeshore, filling pails with shells and pebbles.

They stopped at the kitchen almost every day when Georgie was through with his lessons and chores over at the school, to ask Rosita for bread to feed the hungry ducks. At first Rosita was wary of their trips to the lake.

"Have you asked Robin's grandfather if it's all right?" she would ask.

"I always do," he would answer.

"Do you know what would happen to our boy if you didn't keep an eye on him every minute?"

"Yes, ma'am." To himself he said, "What does she think? Does she think I'm not smart enough to take good care of Robin?"

For the first several times, Mr. Collier went with Georgie when he took Robin down to the lake. Sometimes he stood a short distance from them and watched as they romped in the sand. Occasionally when they went down alone, he would step out from a clump of trees, pretending that he had just happened along. Georgie understood well enough: Mr. Collier was watching him carefully, making sure that Georgie was not the kind of kid who would ever neglect Robin.

Georgie liked having Mr. Collier stop sometimes to hear a few new words Robin had learned to say. "Tell Grandfather who you are, Robin," he would say. Often it would take lots of urging before Robin would answer, then finally he would say, "Robin big boy," and Georgie would smile proudly as he looked up at Mr. Collier.

He thought surely that Mr. Collier would be glad when he heard Robin say a few new words, but there was a strange, sad look in the grandfather's eyes as he picked Robin up in his arms. "Yes, Robin, you're a big boy," he said, but his voice sounded tired as he spoke.

After a while Mr. Collier turned to Georgie. "You are trying hard to help him, Georgie. Paul used to try too. He was very patient with his little brother."

Georgie had wondered about Robin's brother sometimes as he sat in the banyan-tree playhouse. This had been Paul's special place, the hideaway, Georgie had been told, where the Harper boy had come to read or to play at make-believe.

Georgie wondered if Paul would have wanted a strange boy to be in his playhouse, a boy who until recently had not been able to read, who still had shameful welts on his back. And a boy who hated Paul's mother.

There was nothing that pleased Robin so much as feeding the ducks. He grew wildly excited as he watched them approach the shore, eager for their treat, and he squatted and rose repeatedly, making an awkward attempt at jumping up and down. Georgie kept a firm grip on the child's shirt as Robin walked a little way out into the water, screaming partly in delight, partly in fear as one of the ducks snatched at a piece of bread Georgie held out to them.

Georgie had to wait until every duck had given up hope of anything more to eat and had paddled away, before Robin was willing to leave the lakeshore. Robin walked more steadily than he had the year before—Mr. Collier mentioned that—but he still held tightly to Georgie's hand, looking back at the ducks occasionally and babbling happily as he and Georgie approached the banyan tree.

Slowly Georgie began to understand Robin's incoherent attempts at talking which so often puzzled his grandfather. "Do you understand him, Georgie? What is he trying to tell us?" Mr. Collier would often ask and more and more often, Georgie was able to interpret.

"He wants me to build a house for the birds," Georgie reported one day. He shook his head, frowning. "I'm not very good at building things," he said, "I don't think I know how to build a bird house."

"It isn't the house that is important, Georgie—it's the work of building it," Mr. Collier said, and that proved to be true. Robin didn't care that a birdhouse failed to grow out of the scraps of wood Old Eddie found for them; it was enough that he learned, with Georgie's help, to hit a nail so that it would stand, however unsteadily, in one of the pieces of soft wood. The fun of pounding nail after nail while Georgie stood at his side was enough to bring contentment to Robin's world.

More and more often he looked to Georgie for comfort when a finger was hurt, or a knee skinned, or when he was frightened by a sudden thunderbolt. He began to stand at the south side of the garden every afternoon watching for Georgie to appear when the boys came running out of school after classes were over.

For Georgie it was a wonderful thing to know that Robin loved him. He would have gladly spent all of his free hours at Robin's side, but Mr. Collier, watching them play together for hours each day, shook his head. "We can't allow Robin to demand all of your time and attention, Georgie. He loves you, and I'm happy about that, but you must be with boys your own age more often. We hire Amanda to take care of Robin—she can help him feed the ducks and pound nails. You must do things with your friends—"

And so, little by little, Georgie began spending more time at school. Because he was alert and quick, he became a regular on the baseball team made up of the younger boys in school. He enjoyed swimming too, learning quickly with Sister Monica's help. It was in the swimming pool, though, that his first fight in this new school had its beginning.

The boys stripped to their waists when they went into the pool; they beat their chests with Tarzan yells, and felt the hot sun baking their backs browner and browner each day. Sister Monica had never said they must strip to the waist, only that it was all right if they wanted to. Georgie asked if he could wear his shirt and she said O.K.

One day, however, when she was busy at the other end of the pool, Richie Barnes took it upon himself to see that Georgie stripped as the others did.

"Take that shirt off when you come in this pool, fellow," he roared, throwing handfuls of water up into Georgie's face.

"I won't do it," Georgie answered. "It's none of your business about my shirt."

Richie knew how to make his eyes narrow. It gave him a fierce look that worked sometimes with the seven-year-olds when he tried to bully them. "You take that shirt off, you Tampa bum, or I'll take it off for you," he bellowed, approaching Georgie who stepped out of the pool and waited for Richie, his fists clenched.

It wasn't a long fight, but it was a rough one which lasted only until Sister Monica grasped a handful of wet hair on either head and led the combatants inside the gym. When they dried off enough to prevent dripping, she escorted them to Sister Mary Angela's office.

It was the first time Georgie had been led into the office for a scolding. He wouldn't look at Sister Mary Angela.

She was neither angry nor bothered—just cool. "I see you've given Richie a black eye, Georgie. It's rather dangerous and painful to get a black eye, isn't it?"

Georgie knew that she was asking him to remember the many times his own eyes had been dangerously and painfully blackened. He nodded without raising his eyes.

She turned then to Richie. "And people who insist upon butting into other people's business can expect to be roughed up a little, eh, Richie?"

"It was such a dumb thing to get mad about," Richie spluttered. "Sister Monica always tells us we can take off our shirts before we go in the pool. Why does Georgie have to think he's different?"

"Sister Monica tells me that you're a very good swimmer, Richie," she remarked without answering his question.

Richie glowed, black eye and all. "Yes, I am," he acknowledged. "I'm the best in our class."

"Well, if I were a young man who may be swimming in the Olympics someday, I think I'd give my attention to practice rather than trying to boss someone else around about whether or not he wears a shirt while he's in swimming." She leaned her elbows on the desk and regarded the boys frostily. "So—attend to your own business, Mr. Barnes. And you may wear your shirt in the pool, Mr. Burgess. Just be careful about using those fists too freely from now on."

With that she dismissed them, but Sister Monica made them both get dressed and go to their rooms until lunchtime.

That afternoon Timothy and Georgie took a long walk through the woods and finally around to the lake shore. Timothy was thoughtful and sober.

"I know Richie is a stinker, Georgie—all of us think he is when he gets into a mean groove. But I don't understand. Why did you get so mad about that shirt deal?"

"I don't want to talk about it," Georgie answered and walked on with his head lowered.

"I don't blame you for blacking his eye, but I've

been wonderin' about it too. Why do you always wear a shirt in the pool when none of the rest of us do?"

"That's none of your business, Tim." Georgie felt sorry to be talking to Timothy like that, but he had to stop the questioning if he could.

They had reached the banyan tree and seated themselves for a rest in Paul's playhouse.

"I thought me and you was friends, Georgie," Timothy remarked.

"We are," Georgie answered.

"Well, look, if I'm your friend why can't you tell me why wearin' a shirt in the pool is so gosh-awful important to you?"

Georgie looked straight into Timothy's eyes for a long time. Then he slowly made up his mind about something that had never quite lost its terror for him. To Timothy he said, "You won't ever tell?"

"No, of course not."

Georgie drew a long breath. "All right then, I'll show you because you're my friend. But if you ever tell anyone, I'll hate you and I'll never be your friend again—"

As he spoke he slowly unbuttoned his shirt and, throwing it aside, allowed Timothy to see his mutilated back.

Timothy gasped. "What happened to you, Georgie? What made your back like that?"

Georgie swallowed hard before he spoke. "There was a man in Tampa," he said finally, "and he hated me. I was afraid of him and he knowed it—so he liked to hurt me. Ever'time he come to the apartment he took off his belt and whipped me. Sometimes he used a stick. You asked me once how I got my arm hurt—Steve broke it with the leg of a chair he smashed—"

Georgie's heart beat fast. At last he had done it. He had defied his mother's warnings and had dared an invisible Steve to leap out from some hiding place and kill him on the spot. A wave of fear ran through him in spite of the fact that he knew here at the school he was safely hidden from Steve, that there were people around to protect him even if Steve should suddenly appear.

After a minute, though, he felt stronger. He looked up calmly into Timothy's stricken face.

"Didn't your dad and mom call the police, Georgie? Didn't your dad hit the man?" Timothy asked.

"I don't have any dad that I know about. And my mother liked Steve—sometimes she helped him tie me up in the closet—"

"Oh, no—Oh, no—" Timothy could think of

nothing more to say. His own mother loved him a lot—sometimes more than he wanted to be loved when other people were around. His father was dead, but Timothy was able to remember a big man who played games with him, who never failed to bring home a present when he'd been away for a few days.

He stared at Georgie. "I didn't know there was people that mean in all the world," he muttered.

"There is though. Except maybe now Steve's dead. I hope he is."

"I hope so too." They were silent then as Georgie drew on his shirt again.

"But it wasn't your fault, Georgie," Timothy said after a while. "Why couldn't you let the other guys know how it happened? They'd feel as mad about it as I do."

"I guess I'm ashamed." He finished buttoning his shirt and added brusquely, "I still don't like to talk about it, Tim."

They started up the sloping path that led to the Harper's big white house and to the garden no longer forbidden to Georgie or to an occasional friend of his. They didn't say anything at first, then seeing Robin watching them at the gate, they broke into a run to see who could reach him first. Inside the yard, they made a saddle with their clasped hands and gave the delighted little boy a ride around the garden, stopping to admire Georgie's rosebush and to count the red blooms upon it. All of them laughed noisily and yelled at times, but in a secret part of Georgie's mind, everything was quiet and peaceful like the garden was in the early part of night. He was glad that Timothy knew about his back. He was sure that Timothy would never mention it again.

TEN

When Georgie spent time with Robin these days he had many hours in which to watch Old Eddie at work in the garden. Robin could be kept quiet there, happily pounding nail after nail into a piece of wood, and Georgie, taking advantage of such times, paid close attention to every task the old gardener performed. Sometimes he longed to help, but Old Eddie was not happy with boys being what he called "under foot" and so Georgie only watched him from a distance.

One day, however, Mr. Collier made a suggestion. "Would you like to help in the garden now and then, Georgie? Maybe it would be a good thing for you to learn more about taking care of flowers since you like them so much."

Georgie's face showed his eagerness, but a second later he shook his head. "What about Robin? I couldn't keep an eye on him—"

"I think that either Amanda or I can keep an eye on Robin more often. You can romp with him once in a while and take him down to the lake, but as I said before you should be doing other things too—"

Old Eddie was not greatly pleased at first by the idea of having Georgie for a helper. Georgie heard him growl at Mr. Collier as they talked together. "Ain't Sister Mary Angela supposed to keep them kids corralled on the other side of the street?" he said in a mad voice. Then he shrugged and replied to something Mr. Collier said. " Well, then, if Missus wants to turn a kid loose in her garden, I hope she knows what it is she's doin'."

In less than a week, however, Old Eddie and Georgie were working together as if the difference between someone who was almost eight and someone who was seventy had nothing to do with their respect for one another. Georgie, without thinking about it, began to take up some of Old Eddie's movements—shoulders rounded with head leaning forward, a slow shuffling walk in which the front of each foot was thrust forward into the soil at every step.

They didn't talk much, but they soon shared a recognition of what needed to be done and why and when. They drove together into town at intervals and Old Eddie came to depend upon Georgie's memory of what materials were needed for the garden's growth.

Mrs. Harper worked as usual among her favorite flowers, but she kept at some distance from Georgie, seeming never to notice his presence in the garden. One day, however, she spoke to him and that was the day Old Eddie was angered at the behavior of his young helper.

Mrs. Harper was on her way to the tool house after working among the azalea beds. Passing a short distance from Old Eddie and Georgie, she stopped to inspect the edging Georgie had done along one of the flagstone paths. She called out cheerfully, "Nice job you've done here, Georgie. Thank you." Georgie didn't so much as mumble a reply.

Old Eddie was outraged. "Missus only wanted to give you a polite word of thanks," he told Georgie sharply. "Just a polite 'thank you' for somethin' that you'd done to please her. And what did you do? You clammed up and walked away like a loony—that's what you done. If I had the right, I'd give you a good smackin' for your insolence—"

Georgie had nothing to say to Old Eddie either. He carefully raked beneath the hedgerow where he was working, and filled the big wheelbarrow time after time, hauling the debris off to the barrels back of the tool house. After that he silently reproached Mrs. Harper by picking up the recently sharpened pruning shears that she had left lying in the grass the evening before, oiling them, and hanging them in their proper place on the wall of the tool shed.

"Missus is careless—that she is," Old Eddie had told Georgie on other occasions. "A body that neglects good tools never makes an A-1 gardener—" He and Georgie glanced at one another often and shook their heads when they found garden tools that Mrs. Harper had left overnight in the wet grass.

But this day Old Eddie had no praise for Georgie's care of the neglected tools. He kept a severe silence and when Georgie announced that he had finished his work for the day, Old Eddie didn't even bother to glance at him.

Georgie meditated for a long time in the soft shade of a royal poinciana tree before he approached his rosebush. He walked over to sit beside it, heavy-hearted and confused at the war of feelings inside him. For a long while Georgie sat silently, touching its leaves from time to time, but not daring to say anything to his friend.

A curious sparrow stopped to look at the new buds just coming out on the bush and its weight set Georgie's rose swaying over close to him. When the leaves stirred with the swaying, Georgie was almost sure he heard the bush say: "That was a bad thing you done, Georgie."

He sat quietly, listening to all the garden sounds around him. He thought the bush was probably thinking of Mrs. Harper, saying to itself that she was a nice lady and very pretty.

"I say she's mean and ugly," he said sullenly. "I don't care what you think or what Old Eddie thinks either."

The thought suddenly came to him that after all, Mrs. Harper was Robin's mother and that maybe Robin loved her.

For a moment he felt guilty, but that didn't last long. Like a flash he got mad at himself for feeling that way and then he got mad at the rosebush too, and at the world and everybody.

"O.K. So she's his mother. I hate mothers. You

remember the one in Tampa, don't you? Well, I hate her, and I hate Robin's mother too." He paused as a thought occurred to him. "Only she's not really Robin's mother," he whispered. "There are some things around here that you don't know about."

But the rosebush didn't seem at all interested in what Georgie had to say. Georgie was not to be put down, however. "You remember the mean fairy in the story Robin's grandfather read to me when I first started learning?" he asked. "The one that said, 'I'm mad because you didn't invite me so now your child will die,' and the other fairy said, 'Now just hold on a minute. She's not either going to die—she'll simply go to sleep for a hundred years.' You remember the story?"

Several roses nodded in the wind, and Georgie knew the bush was listening closely.

"Well, I'll tell you something," he said. "She stole Robin when he was a baby and she said, 'I'm mad, so I'll put a curse on you. You'll never learn to talk more than a few words—you won't learn to read—or nothin'.'"

He thought he heard the rosebush sigh. It was the way Sister Mary Angela sighed sometimes when she talked to him about forgiving Mrs. Harper. "I suppose you think I'm lyin'," he muttered.

There was no answer. He sat for a long time watching a butterfly trying to make up its mind about something or other as it dashed from one flower to another, circled above a spray of water that had been set to give a bed of tired azaleas a drink, and finally settled on a blade of grass a few inches from Georgie's toes. He watched the slow lift and lowering of the bright wings, smiling to himself.

"Yesterday I learned Robin to say 'butterfly' when we saw one on our walk. His grandfather couldn't understand him, but I could. I said, 'He's sayin' butterfly,' and Mr. Collier told me that I understand Robin better than anybody."

He was silent for a while, thinking to himself about his plans for Robin, but finally he had to tell some of them to his friend. "I'm goin' to keep tryin' till I can learn Robin to talk better. He can say some words real clear already. After that I'll learn him to read—the way Mr. Collier learned me—"

He felt something getting tight in his throat while he was speaking. Finally he said, "I know you don't believe me. You think I can't ever learn Robin to talk except for maybe a few words—you think I'll never learn him to read at all—" He rose and got ready to leave. "Well, you'll see," he said stubbornly, but the tightness still held on in his throat.

Usually he stopped to touch one or more of the roses that toppled on the long stems, or to whisper goodbye and assure his friend that he'd be back soon. But today he felt discouraged and low-spirited. "We're supposed to be friends," he thought, "but it sure don't seem that way right now—" He walked away without saying a word.

Late in the afternoon Georgie took Robin down to the banyan-tree playhouse and on to the lake to feed the ducks. They stopped at the kitchen to ask Rosita for bread and when they left the yard after fastening the big gate behind them, they waved to Mr. Collier, Georgie lifting Robin's hand and showing him how to wave.

When they had thrown the last piece of bread to the ducks, Georgie persuaded Robin to sit beside him in the playhouse. He would have liked to read aloud to the little boy, but Robin would not sit still and listen to reading and so Georgie tried, without very much hope, another method of teaching him.

"See, I'm writing our names here," he said, taking paper and crayon from a niche between two of the tree's many trunks where he left them from one lesson to another. He printed their names in large, straggling letters and tried to get Robin's attention.

"Now here are our names, Robin," he said, feeling

almost sure of failure with his plan, but stubbornly refusing to give up. "This one is yours. When I point here, say your name. Say 'Robin.'"

Robin had been sitting quietly as Georgie printed their names; now suddenly he broke into boisterous laughter, snatching the paper, crumpling and throwing it as far as he could. He pulled Georgie's hair and scratched his forehead; then just as suddenly he returned to his quiet gentleness.

Georgie bent to look into the clouded eyes. "What's the matter with you, Robin? Don't you want me to learn you to read? Don't you know that I was dumb once when I lived in another place and now I read so many books that Sister is surprised?" He took Robin's hand and held it to his cheek. "I don't want kids to call you dumb, Robin."

They sat for a long time after that looking out at the lake which had begun to reflect the colors of sunset. There was a look of shadowy coolness on the surface that made Georgie long to throw his shirt aside and feel the water closing around his body now that there was no one except Robin to see the welts on his back. It wasn't possible though; he had promised Mr. Collier that he'd never go into the lake alone and never would leave Robin by himself.

"But if we had a boat, Robin," he dreamed aloud, "a nice flat old boat all our own, then we could go out there together. We could float around all afternoon and at night we could lay flat in it and look up at the stars. And the good old boat would rock us back and forth, back and forth—"

He made a rocking motion with his hand and Robin took it up, swaying his body from side to side in the motion Georgie's hand had made.

"You understood that, didn't you, Robin? You knowed what I meant when I said, 'back and forth' just as well as anyone—" He was pleased at any sign of understanding on Robin's part. Mr. Collier had said, "We mustn't expect too much, Georgie; we must be glad of any strides Robin is able to make, no matter how small they are."

After a while, however, he grew uneasy as Robin's rocking motion continued, and he frowned as he watched the child who seemed to have forgotten that Georgie sat beside him. "That's enough," he said, "that's enough to show me that you understand." Finally he spoke with unaccustomed sharpness. "Stop it, Robin," and with that the rocking motion stopped and Robin looked up at him, seeming to wonder at his tone.

A few minutes later he heard the sound of Old

Eddie's truck coming down the road which led from the north end of the garden. Georgie watched its approach and the uncomfortable feeling he had known since Old Eddie's angry words in the garden returned to make him feel worried and uncertain. He felt the loss of a friendship that had comforted him for many months.

"Me and you are artists, Georgie," Old Eddie had told him once. "Missus pointed that up to me a long time ago. We give the bushes fair, neat shapes, we bring out the best in a passel of flowers with the right fertilizer and the right amount of water, we scotch the weeds and kill the insects that are hurtful—so ain't she right? Ain't me and you artists same as if we held brushes in our hands?"

Georgie had liked that, except that he chose not to remember that the idea came from Mrs. Harper. It was pleasant, though, to think that his work in the garden was something like an artist's work, just as his book work with Mr. Collier was something like a writer's work.

When the truck was within a short distance of the banyan tree, Georgie raised his hand timidly in greeting. He was half afraid Old Eddie would ignore him as he had done earlier, half afraid that he might stop and continue with the earlier scolding.

But the old man waved, seeming friendly enough, and stopping his truck on the shoulder of the road, he climbed down from the driver's seat, grimacing at some pain in his legs. He walked up to the playhouse and leaned against one of the tree trunks.

"Thought I'd best stop and tell you I'm not mad," he said, looking over Georgie's head at the woods beyond.

Georgie ducked his head in the gesture he had almost given up lately. Sister Mary Angela didn't believe that a ducked head was an acceptable substitute for a polite word, but at that moment Georgie could think of no polite word.

Old Eddie struck a match and held it to the bowl of his pipe, sucking noisily at the stem. "I oughtn't to said I'd like to smack you, Georgie. Missus and me done some talkin' after you left this afternoon, and now I re'lize that you've been smacked too much already in your life. Still and all, you was hateful to her and she's had too much grief in her life like you've had too much smackin' in yours—"

Georgie thought of the things he had heard from Sister Mary Angela about Mrs. Harper's grief. "Her boy got killed, didn't he?" Georgie asked, knowing it well but wanting to hear more about it from Old Eddie.

"Her little boy and her man," Old Eddie answered soberly, and Georgie felt a great curiosity to hear what Old Eddie might tell him about Robin's brother.

"Did you like Paul?" he asked after a while.

"Ever'body liked Paul. He was bright and lively—about your age, I'd say—maybe a little older—Missus used to come down here to this very spot with him and they'd read together. Sometimes we'd hear 'em up in the garden, laughin' over some story they both liked. Missus doted on that boy—it's the truth."

Georgie felt a deep, aching jealousy growing inside him because Mrs. Harper had come down to the play-house to read with Paul—because she would never, never come down here to read with Georgie. He felt guilty too, because he was jealous of this boy Mrs. Harper had loved—this Paul who had had everything, but was now dead.

Then a new thought occurred to him. "She liked Paul better than Robin, didn't she?" he asked.

Old Eddie thought for a minute before he answered. "There's differ'nt feelin's mixed up in lovin' kids," he said finally. "Bein' proud of a child they know is a-goin' to shine in the world and havin' folks say, 'That there fine young fellow's your boy, ain't he?'—well, that's one kind of love. But knowin' pity and at the same time holdin' up for the one that ain't ever goin' to shine—lookin' straight at the world and sayin' 'This here is my boy too'—that's another kind of love. Maybe it's more unselfish to be proud of the second one—I don't rightly know."

A blue heron waded majestically up toward the shore of the lake and stood some distance away, staring at the three figures near the shore. Georgie and Old Eddie watched it absently; Robin clapped his hand once and then resumed his look of quiet dreaming.

After a while Old Eddie turned to go back to his truck. "Well, you come over tomorrow same as usual, Georgie. Me and you ought to finish trimmin' that hedge before we go on with the mowin'," he said.

Georgie waved as Old Eddie drove away; then he led Robin toward the house. He was glad when Mr. Collier came down to the gate and lifted the child in his arms. "You have a tired boy with you this evening, haven't you, Georgie?"

Georgie nodded. He was conscious that Mrs. Harper was watching him from the patio, but he made no sign of recognition, hurrying away instead and taking a path far to the west of the house on his way back to the school.

When he came to the rosebush he stopped for a minute, touching the clustered leaves and stroking a half-opened bud that looked at him sleepily in the deepening twilight. He felt an air of reproach in his friend and he longed to set things right.

"Don't be mad," he said finally. "We've got to be good to each other, the way we always was before. Maybe some day—I thought when Old Eddie talked about her, that maybe some day—" He left the sentence hanging, not knowing exactly what it was he wanted to say.

ELEVEN

From time to time Sister Mary Angela called a group of boys from the same class into her office for refreshments and a report on their school activities. She taught only music classes, but as Director of the school she liked to keep in touch with the boys. It was an hour everybody in Georgie's class enjoyed.

"We like braggin' to Sister about how smart we are," Timothy told Georgie when the first meeting of the year was called, "and at the same time havin' all the cracker and peanut butter sandwiches we want in the middle of the afternoon."

Sister Mary Angela listened attentively to everything they had to tell her that afternoon. Timothy had a science experiment going—running white rats in a maze he had built himself, rewarding them for making a correct turn with the sound of musical chimes, punishing them for wrong turns with a clash of cymbals.

"Then I'll compare their learning time with another group rewarded with food and punished with no food. I predict the food-rewarded ones will do best—I know I would," he added, accepting his fifth sandwich and grinning at Sister Mary Angela.

Richie had read an article on power conservation and reported on it in some detail, Tom Wilcox told about a recent field trip to an orange grove and a talk with the orchardist; Kevin had written some poetry which he handed to Sister, asking if she would please read it in private and talk to him about it later. Georgie sat quietly listening and saying nothing.

After a while, quite out of the blue, Sister asked, "Now, what about books? What have you boys been reading lately?"

Timothy immediately pointed to Georgie. "Ask him, Sister. He's the one with his nose in a book half of the time."

She turned to Georgie, smiling. "All right, then,

let's hear from the book-lover. What books have you liked best lately, Georgie?"

Her words took him back painfully to another classroom. "What do you like best?" Miss Cressman had asked. He had been afraid to answer at first, but finally he said, "I like flowers," and then he felt hot and ashamed. The kids had giggled when they saw that Georgie was ashamed and he could still feel the lonesomeness of that moment.

But things were different now. These kids were his friends, especially Timothy, and Sister Mary Angela's smile was like her—gentle and nice. Still the memories that hurt him were too sharp for him to speak; they made his face grow hot and his throat begin to tighten.

"Won't you name just a few of them, Georgie? I'd like to know if there are some I've missed and maybe have a treat coming—"

Georgie took a deep breath then and looked at her. "Well, I liked, *The Moonsinger* and all the fairy tales—especially 'The Ugly Duckling.' And then I liked *The Miraculous Pitcher* and *Bambi*. I wanted to read *Treasure Island* but it's a little too hard for me." He paused and then added hurriedly, "Oh, yes, another one—a real old one that Mr. Collier found for me. It's called *A Dog of Flanders*—"

Sister Mary Angela leaned forward. "Oh, Georgie, I read that book when I was a little girl and I cried so hard my father was upset and told the teacher that I should have only cheerful books to read until I was older. I guess he didn't know that I liked to cry over certain books—"

He nodded to her with a message in his eyes. He wanted to tell her that he too had cried over Nello and Patrashe when he was alone in his room.

When the meeting was about over, Sister spoke to them about her choir. "I'm in need of some treble voices," she told them. "My choirboys grow up before I know it—most of the treble voices in the choir are changing so fast from high to low that we are getting top-heavy with deep voices." She glanced around the group. "Anybody care to come up to the organ loft tomorrow after classes and try out?"

Richie and Timothy raised their hands immediately and several of the other boys followed their lead. Kevin shook his head. "Not me, Sister. I can't keep a tune going right to save my neck—" Georgie didn't raise his hand, but in answer to her questioning look, he said, "I don't know if I could do it—I'd like to if I thought I could learn—"

"Come up with Timothy tomorrow and we'll

find out whether I think you can learn or not—" She passed the last sandwiches around and shooed the boys out of her office.

The next afternoon Timothy and Georgie were the first two ready for the try-outs. Sister Mary Angela made a little running tune on the organ and asked Timothy to repeat it with the syllable she gave him.

"Pretty good, Tim," she commented. "Come in for practice tomorrow afternoon."

When it was Georgie's turn she tested him in the same way, and after he had done his best, she played another short tune and asked him to try again. She did that a third time and just when he was sure that he had failed, she turned and placed her hand on his shoulder.

"You were born with a musical gift, Georgie. You have what we call perfect pitch." She looked pleased. "Come in for practice with Tim. You two will fit in very well with the older boys."

The hours of choir practice were joyful ones for Georgie. It was a proud moment when he and the other new additions to the choir had learned a chorale well enough to sing the next day with the older boys.

"My voice helped make the singing beautiful," he

told his rosebush after the first session with the entire choir. "Sister says our trebles are first-rate—she is proud of us—"

It rained intermittently for several days during the week Sister Mary Angela prepared to have her newly organized choir sing in the chapel on Friday evening.

Timothy and Georgie were walking back to their rooms from the playground on the gloomy afternoon before their first appearance as choirboys when they saw Molly Harper walking slowly in her garden with Robin at her side. Her face looked tired and sad, Georgie noticed, and for a few seconds he felt sorry for her.

Timothy waved his hand and called out a cheerful greeting to her.

Molly looked over at them and smiled tiredly. "Hello, boys. What has happened to our sunlight lately?"

Timothy stepped up to the street curb, eager to talk to her; Georgie held back, his eyes fixed on the ground. He knew what Old Eddie would have said if he had been there—"You're actin' like a loony, young man"—but loony or not, he couldn't bring himself to talk as Timothy did.

"We're singing a Bach chorale at vespers tonight,

Mrs. Harper," Timothy told her. "I'm not sure if you know that Georgie and me are in the choir now. Why don't you bring Robin and come over to hear us?"

She came up to the fence and laid her hands on the pickets. "Yes, Timothy, Father heard you boys practicing the other day—he told me that I should come over and hear you—" She could not tell them that after her father's urging she had said to Rosita, "I don't think I'm quite healed enough to hear nine-year-old voices singing a Bach chorale—"

"Well, then why don't you make us a visit?" Timothy urged. "Sister is real glad to have people come in to hear our music."

Molly looked down at Robin and fondled his hand. "Would you like to go over to Georgie's school with Mother and hear the boys sing?" she asked, and when Robin's face showed his delight, she turned again to Timothy. "Robin thinks the school belongs exclusively to Georgie," she said. Then she added, "Thank you for the invitation, Timothy. I'll think about it."

"She'll be over, I'm pretty sure," Timothy said as he and Georgie walked on together. "When they say 'I'll think about it' they mean yes. Anyway, she looks awful lonesome."

Georgie felt a sadness inside him. He knew what it meant to be lonesome, and he thought it must be very sad to have Paul and his father dead. He knew too, however, that he could never forget the morning Mrs. Harper screamed at him, threatening his rosebush or the wild, mean dreams he'd had of her when his fever was high. He felt as if two Georgies were fighting inside him, one pushing in a certain direction, the other quickly pushing back in the other.

His heart pounded that evening as he pulled his choir-robe on and then stood before Sister Mary Angela who adjusted the white collar and brushed his hair smoothly across his forehead before going down the row to perform the same service for each boy.

"She will hear me sing—maybe she will know my voice is helping to make it beautiful—" He tried hard to remember that he didn't care whether she heard him or not, that her thinking he was good meant nothing at all to him.

The chill outside made the chapel seem warm and friendly that evening. There were lighted candles on the organ and when Mrs. Harper came in she brought a great basket of late flowers from her garden which Sister Dolores accepted and placed at the feet of the choirboys in the front row. They filled the organ loft with fragrance.

Mrs. Harper looked very beautiful as she sat with Robin near the front of the chapel. Her long braids were twisted into a crown around her head as if for a very special occasion, and she wore a soft-looking dress of blue silk with gold flowers on her high collar. Georgie had never seen her except in the careless work clothes she wore in the garden.

"She dressed up nice for us," he thought and caught his breath as he looked at her. Then he fixed his eyes upon Sister Mary Angela and kept his thoughts on the chorale the choir was going to sing.

Every boy sat unmoving and watchful until at a sign from Sister Mary Angela they rose, faces alert, eyes never moving from her. The organ whispered a low command and they sang, sweetly and beautifully, obeying Sister's every direction. At first the voices were soft and quietly reverent, then they swelled with power as the tones of the organ swelled. The chorale became so strong and rich that Georgie felt his rose must be hearing it over in the garden. Finally the voices and the organ grew softer and softer until there was only a breath of music at the end.

When the choir had allowed the last note to fade

away, Georgie stole a glance at Mrs. Harper. She was crying.

When the brief service was over the choirboys filed out of a side door from the organ loft and stood in a small room off the foyer until the student body had marched out into the front hall. Sister Mary Angela stood with them and when she saw Mrs. Harper approaching, she hurried toward her with outstretched hands.

"It was good of you to come over this evening, Mrs. Harper. Do come in and say a word to my choirboys—they are very pleased that you came over to hear them sing."

"I came to thank them, Sister. Their singing was beautiful—very close to being magnificent. It made me cry, but I feel better for having heard them—" The boys were crowding around her, proud of their accomplishment, ready to bask in her praise. Georgie stood in the background, allowing himself to be hidden by the older boys in the crowded room. Once he ventured near enough that he could have touched her dress, but he would not say one word to attract her attention. He patted Robin's head briefly and the child prattled an attempt to say his name. But Georgie could not talk to Robin there and so he withdrew to the farthest point in the room and tried not to wonder if she had recognized him in his handsome robe, if she had heard his voice with something called a perfect pitch blending in with the others.

A few days later Sister Mary Angela called all of the eight- and nine-year-old boys into her office for a special announcement.

"How would you like to study dramatics and perhaps give a play later on before the student body?" she asked.

There was a wild and enthusiastic response. Georgie was excited and delighted at the prospect; he had gone with Sister Mary Angela and a dozen other boys earlier in the fall to see a production of *Pinocchio* at the children's theatre in a neighboring town. He had sat, hardly breathing, as he watched children no older than himself perform a story-book miracle on the stage. He had dreamed about that vivid, first experience for weeks afterward.

"A lot of work is involved," Sister Mary Angela was saying. "Classes will have to be held after school hours and that will mean you may have to give up other activities that you enjoy if you enter the dramatics class. It won't be altogether a lark—there will be hard work and some sacrifices to be made—"

"Are you going to teach us, Sister?" Timothy asked curiously as a small suspicion began to grow in his mind.

"No, Tim. Mrs. Harper will teach the new class. And for this first term, she wants to work with boys your age. I think you may probably know why—"

"Paul?" Timothy said quickly.

"Yes. Because of Paul." Sister Mary Angela answered. She stopped for a minute and seemed to be thinking. Then she said, "When Mrs. Harper heard the boys' choir the other night she began to wonder if maybe it would make her feel better if she could work with boys who were Paul's age. She didn't know, at first, what kind of work she could do, but when we talked it over we thought that since she is an actress, she might teach you boys how to act out stories— maybe put on a play for the older boys—"

There was enthusiastic yelling at Sister Mary Angela's words. Georgie didn't yell. He knew that Sister Mary Angela was looking at him, but he wouldn't look back at her.

"Of course you can do as you please about taking the class," Sister Mary Angela said. "Some of you may be more interested in other things. Some of you may not care about acting, but would like to build sets or paint scenery—there are so many things to be done besides acting when we put on a play, and we want this to be a pleasant experience for everybody—"

Then she told the boys that Mr. Collier would be writing dramatized versions of scenes from various books for their class. "He is coming over every day for the next week or so and will read to you so that you'll be familiar with the stories you are acting out. He will read parts of *Treasure Island*, of *Tom Sawyer*, several scenes from *Alice in Wonderland*—maybe some poems which he thinks would be fun for you to dramatize—Mrs. Harper mentioned *The King's Breakfast* which Paul used to like so much."

Georgie sat in on the reading sessions. Boys crowded so close to Mr. Collier that his head was only a spot of silver among the black and brown, red and blond heads around him. His voice was lively, often full of laughter or ominous with predictions of disaster as he read the great old stories to them. When Georgie listened to Tom Sawyer slyly luring the boys into white washing the fence for Aunt Polly, or to the bloody pirates talking while Jim Hawkins listened as he lay crouched in the apple-barrel, he was half sick with the longing to join Mrs. Harper's class. He had not yet read *Alice in Wonderland*, but as the White

Rabbit, the Duchess, the Hatter and Alice as well as a dozen others became real and living characters, Georgie could hardly stay with his decision never to be friendly with Mrs. Harper.

"I wish she hadn't been mean," he thought to himself. "I wish she hadn't pulled up my rosebush or said the things she did. I wish I didn't have to keep her for my enemy—"

Once Sister Mary Angela spoke to him privately about the dramatics class. "You sing so well, Georgie, and you enjoy singing, don't you?"

"Yes, ma'am, I like to sing—if you're the one that teaches us."

"Now that you know you can do things well— you've learned to read and to sing—don't you think it would be fun to be in a play? Mrs. Harper has told me that she'd be happy to have you in her class—"

There was the same sullen shake of his head when Mrs. Harper's name was mentioned. Sister Mary Angela's face took on a look of tiredness as she watched him turn away from her.

"The tire is still spinning in the icy rut, isn't it, Georgie? It's still cutting deeper and deeper and getting positively nowhere—"

Later he sat beside his rosebush and sulked.

"Never—never—never—" was all he could manage to say. Then remembering the crowd of boys in the auditorium yelling with delight at being accepted in the class, he added, "Bunch of dumb idiots—" and told himself that he had better things to do than act in a play.

TWELVE

The boys who didn't care to try out for roles in the skits Mrs. Harper was directing were given the privilege of sitting in the auditorium during rehearsals and listening to the others. Many of these observers planned to help with scenery, to print programs, or to become part-time stage managers.

Georgie Burgess planned to do nothing in connection with the drama class, but during the first few weeks after the beginning of the class, he never missed a single rehearsal period.

Everything about the stage directions fascinated him—how a change of tone or a facial expression was worth any number of words, how every aside, supposedly muttered, must, all the same, be enunciated so that no one in the audience missed it.

He listened to the lines of each skit and learned them, certain in some cases that his own delivery of them in the seclusion of his room was better than that of the struggling actors trying to follow Mrs. Harper's directions.

When he knew all the lines perfectly, Georgie stopped sitting in on rehearsals and went down to the banyan-tree playhouse to be an actor all by himself. Timothy, however, kept him supplied with gossip from the dressing room of the auditorium. "You know how gung ho Kevin was about gettin' the part of Alice in the Mad Tea Party?" Timothy asked one evening as he and Georgie sat on the front steps and talked together. "Well, now, he ain't so sure. He's beginning to get scared of wearin' a dress and a girl-wig in front of all the big guys in school."

"He oughta thought about that a long time ago," Georgie remarked wisely; then he turned to face Timothy. "Would you take the part of Alice, Tim?"

"If I had one speck of a chance, I would. Mrs. Harper gets real sore at guys that are afraid to take girl roles. She said, 'Look, in the olden days all the roles of ladies was took by boys.' She says it's stupid to laugh about it, and if anyone does, she's goin' to bounce him out of the play—just like that." Timothy snapped his fingers to show the speed with which Mrs. Harper would carry out her threat. "She'd do it too," he continued. "I like her and she's O.K., but boy, can she be tough!"

Georgie silently agreed. He had reason to remember when Mrs. Harper had been tough.

"I wish you'd tried out for a part, Georgie," Timothy said after a while. "You'd make a much better John Silver than Larry Lawrence does. Larry's afraid to let himself go, and like Mrs. Harper says, if you're John Silver you got to behave like a pirate. I don't see why you didn't try out for one of the roles. So you don't like Mrs. Harper—O.K.; so you bite off your nose to spite your face."

"I just don't like plays," Georgie lied evenly. "I couldn't stand actin' in a stupid play."

"Well, I like 'em," Timothy answered and continued complacently. "I not only like 'em, but I'm pretty good in 'em too. Mrs. Harper says my White Rabbit—the one that's late for his appointment with the Duchess—is real good. I saw her grin and wink at Sister Dolores once when I was goin' strong."

After a while it seemed that all of his friends, boys and adults as well, were involved one way or another in the drama class. Sister Dolores was helping Mrs. Harper in a dozen ways, Mr. Collier was busy writing more skits for the following term, Rosita was sewing costumes. Even Amanda apparently knew what was going on.

"My lands, Georgie," she teased one afternoon, "why is your face so long these days? You kickin' yourself for not takin' part in one of the plays over at your school?"

He gave Amanda a cold look and walked on with Robin down to the playhouse. "I could be in one of the silly plays if I wanted to, Robin—I know all of the lines. I could be Tom Sawyer or Jim Hawkins or John Silver or the Mad Hatter. I could be Alice too, and I wouldn't be afraid to wear a dress and a girl-wig either. But I won't. I wouldn't be in one of her plays if she coaxed me for a year—she couldn't make me be in one of them—"

Once when Mr. Collier paid Georgie and Robin an unexpected call at the playhouse, he found Georgie delivering the lines of one skit after another, working with pretended props, changing from a scowling pirate to a scheming Tom Sawyer with apparent ease. Robin sat quietly watching with a puzzled expression as if this new Georgie amazed him.

Mr. Collier clapped lightly as Georgie finished whitewashing an imaginary fence and sat down beside Robin.

"That was very good, Georgie. Can you do the Mad Tea Party for me?"

Georgie was too pleased by the grandfather's praise to show the usual sullenness that appeared whenever the plays were mentioned. Without hesitation he became a Mad Hatter, a March Hare, a Dormouse, and a confused Alice. It was fun. He forgot to be shy or afraid as he often was. He even forgot that he was Georgie Burgess.

At the end of the performance, Mr. Collier frowned slightly with a puzzled look on his face. "I can't understand, Georgie. Why did you learn all these lines and gestures and stage behavior if you don't like plays and don't want to act in them?"

Georgie flushed as he saw Mr. Collier watching him try to find an answer. "I just learned 'em to say to Robin," he said finally. "I wouldn't do 'em on a stage— I don't like acting on a stage—"

Mr. Collier looked as if he understood. "Yes, many people feel that way about appearing before an audience. I have to admit that I've always had a secret wish to be an actor though I'm afraid I've never stood much of a chance of being one—" He motioned to a seat beside Robin, inviting Georgie to sit and talk for a while. "Tell me, which one of the skits is the best in your opinion?"

"The Mad Tea Party," Georgie answered without hesitation. "That one is more fun than any of them—especially the Mad Hatter. He's real funny—crazy too."

The grandfather's voice was grave as he answered. "Yes, the Mad Tea Party is a thing to love while you're young—to still love when you're as old as I am. It means something very special to my daughter, a great deal more than do any of the others."

Georgie was curious. "Why does she like that one best?" he asked, wondering at the sadness on Mr. Collier's face.

"Paul had a Mad Tea Party role in his school play the first year we came down here. He was the most pleased and excited boy I ever saw when he came home and told us that he'd been chosen for the Mad Hatter—"

The old jealousy rose inside Georgie and with it the old sense of guilt that he was jealous of a dead boy. "Was he a good Hatter?" he asked in a small voice.

Mr. Collier nodded, barely smiling. "Yes. We all helped him with his role—his mother was Alice, his daddy and I took the roles of the March Hare and the Dormouse. I remember that sometimes our foolish expressions would make Paul forget he was an actor and he'd crack up in the midst of his lines—"

"Robin couldn't have a part, could he?"

"No, but his parents saw to it that Robin was included in the fun whenever he wanted to be. Occasionally he'd come up babbling something that seemed to say he wanted to be in the play too; one of us would pick him up—help him pretend at pouring tea or at listening to the Hatter's big watch tick. We were always careful to see that Robin had a chance to join in Paul's fun once in a while."

"I'm glad," Georgie said in a low voice.

Mr. Collier looked out across the lake and when he spoke, the words seemed to be said to himself.

"It was hard for her to do the Mad Tea Party with the boys over at the school. But she did—in spite of her memories. My girl is a very brave lady—"

It was the first time Georgie fully realized that Mrs. Harper was Mr. Collier's "girl"—that maybe he loved Robin's mother the way Sister Mary Angela's father loved her when he said, "No more sad stories for my child until she's older—" Inside his mind, Georgie was saying, "I wish—I wish—" but his mind couldn't quite tell him what it was he wished.

That night he dreamed about being in a play—talking on a stage in front of a large audience, among them, a tall rosebush. He heard Mrs. Harper say, "You're good, Georgie—you're very good."

Then suddenly there was trouble about the Mad Tea Party. Timothy told Georgie all about it. "You know I told you what she'd do to any guy that teased Kevin about taking the role of Alice? Want to know what happened?"

"Yes. What did?"

"It wasn't any big surprise. Richie had been grinnin' all week about Kevin wearin' a dress when he plays Alice. Well, today, he had to tease him or bust—so he did, and Kevin hit him. Richie's front tooth got run through his lip—and besides that, Mrs. Harper bounced him out of the play—" Timothy shrugged in callous disregard for Richie's trouble.

Georgie's heart gave an unreasoning leap. He knew, of course, that there was not the slightest chance that Mrs. Harper would call upon a sullen, loony-behaving Georgie to take the part, no matter if her father had told her how well he had said the lines down at the banyan tree. Still, Georgie couldn't help asking, "Couldn't she find someone else to take the Hatter's role in Richie's place?"

"Wouldn't do any good," Timothy answered, "'cause after he'd punched Richie, Kevin got to cryin' and sayin' he couldn't play Alice, and after a while he got so worked up that he puked all over the dressing-room floor and Mrs. Harper told Sister Mary Angela no, that she wouldn't ask another guy to dress like Alice because we ain't mature enough. So—alas, alas—there ain't no Alice either." Timothy grinned at his friend, happily indifferent about the folding of the skit. Timothy didn't know, Georgie thought, that the Mad Tea Party meant more to Mrs. Harper than any other one of the skits.

During the following days there was considerable grousing among the boys over the cancellation of the Mad Tea Party. Reports had leaked out that it was the best of all the skits to be presented; there was general disappointment. But Mrs. Harper was unmoved. "No," she said to the few who asked her if she couldn't find someone to fill the vacant roles, "I don't think so. We'll have to wait until some gentlemen around here learn that girls' roles are just as good as theirs—sometimes considerably better—"

"I'd take a girl's role for her—I know I could do it," Georgie thought, but Mrs. Harper wasn't asking any favors, and nothing could have made Georgie suggest the possibility to her.

He listened forlornly to Timothy's account of other troubles in the drama class. Rosita, it seemed, had made a mistake in measuring Larry for his John Silver costume and when it turned out to be so small that the vicious old pirate couldn't get into it, he threw a very childish tantrum in front of the whole class.

There was the case too of Ross Davis who couldn't project his voice or enunciate his lines distinctly. Timothy chuckled as he told Georgie about it. "Every time he says his lines Sister Dolores sings out from the back of the auditorium, 'Louder, Ross; we can't understand a word back here—' And sometimes Ross looks like he wants to go out and drown himself—"

Georgie followed Sister Mary Angela into the organ loft the day before the skits were to be given, and listened without the pleasure he usually felt as she played the music that helped her to rest and relax.

When she was through playing, she looked down at him where he sat beside the organ bench. "Is my boy unhappy these days?" she asked quietly.

"Yes, Sister."

"Do you want to tell me about it?"

He tried to organize his troubled thoughts. Then he said, "Did you know that Paul was the Mad Hatter in a play one time?"

"Yes," she answered soberly. "The Harpers and Mr. Collier invited Sister Dolores and me to go with him into town that night to see Paul's school play. It was delightful," she added.

"He was good, wasn't he?"

"Very good," she agreed. "His parents were terribly proud of him."

Georgie said nothing more and Sister Mary Angela sat quietly. The sunlight sifted into the loft and fell on Georgie's face. Outside the yells of boys on the playground were shrill and loud; across the street the buzz of Old Eddie's lawn mower could be heard as he rode around and around the wide lawn that surrounded Mrs. Harper's house.

"Sister, I wish—I hadn't ever hated her," Georgie said after the silence between them had lasted for many minutes.

She looked down at him, but she didn't speak. Georgie tried again to say what he wanted very much to say.

"I wish I'd told her I'd be in her class—maybe if I

had, she would of made me the Hatter and I wouldn't of laughed at Kevin and the Tea Party wouldn't of been spoiled for her—"

"I wish that too, Georgie. Lots of things might have been different, but then, it's too late to think about it now." She rose, getting ready to go back to her work. "Why don't you go over and tell her that you wish you had never hated her?"

Georgie shook his head. "I just can't do it," he said miserably.

Sister Mary Angela rearranged some books of music on the organ. "Then would you like for me to tell her?" she asked.

For the life of him, Georgie couldn't say yes as he wanted to say; instead he muttered, "If you want to, you can," and his face grew red when Sister Mary Angela said, "Oh, Georgie, Georgie, that was a left-handed yes, wasn't it?"

The next morning everybody except Georgie was getting ready for the first production of the drama class. There was persistent hammering in the auditorium and a shouting of commands among the workers. Rosita came hurrying over, her arms loaded with costumes she'd just finished; Sister Dolores was in the dressing room helping a couple of late-learners with their lines; Timothy was stationed at the stage door forbidding any of the older boys to peek inside at what was going on.

Georgie wandered from one spot to another and was painfully aware that no one—not Sister Mary Angela, not Timothy, not Mrs. Harper—paid any attention to him. Finally he went into the front parlor where he curled up in an armchair, trying to read a new book he'd found in the library and discovering that he somehow had lost his taste for reading that morning.

Mr. Collier found him there in mid-morning, and drew up a chair beside him.

"Georgie, Sister Mary Angela told my daughter and me something last night that pleased us very much—she said that you wished you had taken part in her class earlier."

Georgie looked down at the floor, but Mr. Collier's next words brought his eyes up quickly. "Do you think you could do the Mad Hatter if my daughter gave you a rehearsal with the rest of the cast this afternoon?"

All the last traces of his resentment toward Mrs. Harper melted before the bright light of that moment. Georgie's face glowed as he answered.

"Yes, sir, I'll do it. I know I can."

"I know you can too—I remember how well you did the parts for me that day down at the playhouse. I'm not worried about that."

"Are you worried about Alice? Can't she find anybody to take that part?"

"I believe that problem is settled. No," Mr. Collier looked at Georgie thoughtfully, "I want to be certain you can bring yourself to forget your trouble with my daughter, Georgie—can you?"

"I already have."

"I believe you, but I wanted to hear you say it. All right, I'll tell her that you'll take the part if she feels you can manage it." He got up and walked away hurriedly.

The first three skits presented that evening were received with high enthusiasm by the audience. Timothy, as the White Rabbit, was convincing in his terrible worry over being late for an appointment with the Duchess, and earned a special round of applause for himself. Tom Sawyer received waves of appreciative laughter throughout his performance as a master con man, and Larry as Long John Silver in a costume completely done over by Rosita brought down the house with a display of his chilling wickedness. Then when Sister Dolores stepped out from the wing and announced that the Mad Tea Party would be given after all, the student body applauded wildly.

Through a crack in the curtains Georgie and Timothy could see the expectant audience before them. Mr. Collier sat well up in front with Rosita on one side of him and Sister Mary Angela on the other; Robin was on his lap leaning within the circle of his grandfather's arm. Old Eddie and his wife sat farther down in the same row with Amanda. Timothy proudly pointed out his mother to Georgie—"She drove all the way down from Jacksonville just to see me do the White Rabbit," he whispered to Georgie.

When the curtains parted for the Tea Party the audience buzzed in surprise at seeing Georgie Burgess seated at the tea table, high hat and tall collar identifying him as the Mad Hatter. But as the Hatter, the March Hare, and the Dormouse looked out toward the right wing and began to clamor that there was no room for an approaching girl at the tea table, Molly Harper stepped out of the wing, and the room erupted with a delighted roar.

This was an Alice the boys hadn't expected to see. She was wearing a short dress with a crepe-paper pinafore that Rosita had pinned together less than an hour before. Her hair was loosed from the well-known braids and fell back of her shoulders in a heavy golden fall held from her forehead by a velvet band. She was more beautiful than they had ever seen her before and the play was delayed for a time by the audience's loud enthusiasm.

When finally the dialogue began and the Hatter, looking critically at Alice, remarked in carefully enunciated syllables, "You know, your hair wants cutting," the audience broke out in laughter and someone shouted, "No. No, Georgie. Mrs. Harper's hair doesn't want cutting."

It was soon evident that Georgie had attended carefully during the hours when he sat at the back of the auditorium watching rehearsals and listening to Mrs. Harper's comments and directions. He forgot a boy named Georgie completely once the play opened and became a ridiculously pompous old Hatter who teased Alice and irritated her with his sly mockery.

The saucy lines which a Georgie Burgess behind the Hatter's big spectacles dared to say openly to the Molly Harper behind Alice's pinafore tickled the audience immensely. When the March Hare asked her please to have more wine and she replied angrily that since she hadn't had any yet, she couldn't very well take more, the Hatter was impudent.

"You mean you can't take less," he said smugly. "It's very easy to take more than nothing."

And when he waved his arms in an extravagant gesture as he recited, "Twinkle, twinkle, little bat, how I wonder where you're at," Alice looked at him in what was surely puzzled disbelief, and the audience howled at a Georgie Burgess they had never known before.

It was fun, heady exciting fun. As the curtains began to close, Georgie wished desperately that the skit had not ended so soon. He looked up at Mrs. Harper and, under the stress of his excitement and the din of applause in the auditorium, he dared to speak to her of his feelings.

"I wish we had words for an hour longer," he said.

She laughed at that almost as gaily as Sister Mary Angela sometimes laughed. "Grease paint gets into one's blood, Georgie," she said.

He didn't quite understand her words, but he was glad he'd had the courage to speak to her as Georgie rather than as the Hatter.

At the curtain call the four Tea Party characters came out hand in hand. They bowed graciously to the audience; then as Mrs. Harper turned and stood facing the three boys, she bowed and smiled at them and they returned the courtesy. It looked very friendly; Georgie hoped it looked something like Paul's curtain call a long time ago.

Boys by the dozen crowded around Molly Harper when the program was over, loud in their compliments. Georgie stood for a moment, wanting to speak to her, but still too shy to break through the crowd pressing around her. Instead, he slipped out a side door, hurried across the street and opened the big gate at the entrance to the garden.

He sat down beside his rosebush trembling with excitement and a happiness that left him giddy.

"I talked to her," he whispered. "She asked me did I want to play the Hatter and I said yes. She looked at me for a long time and then she said all right, but would I be in the play if she took the part of Alice and I said I would. Then I asked her but wasn't she too big and she laughed and told me to remember the little cakes that made Alice grow big when she ate them—"

The rosebush looked more beautiful in the moonlight than he had ever seen it before.

"I was good—I know I was," he continued. "I said the lines and never stumbled. Sister Dolores was in the wing waitin' to give me a cue if I needed it, but I didn't—not once. I said the lines the way the Hatter would of said them, and Mrs. Harper thought that I was good—I didn't ask her, but I just knowed it—" He paused and for a long time he didn't speak. Finally he drew a leaf down where he could look at it closely. "I liked her tonight," he said in a very low voice. "I liked her a lot. I wished she was my mother same as she is to Robin and to the boy that died—"

"Maybe she is, Georgie," the rosebush seemed to whisper so faintly that Georgie was not quite sure he heard what it said.

He felt a shiver go through his body. "Maybe she is," he said softly, not daring to say the words that were in his mind. "Maybe in a time before I can remember there was a fairy that was mad and took me away from her and give me to mean people for a long time till finally—till finally, there was a play and there was me and my mother bein' Alice and the Hatter in it together—"

He sat unmoving, listening to the night sounds in the garden. He saw Mr. Collier and Rosita walking slowly across the street with Robin between them and Amanda following close behind. Later he heard the din of his classmates' voices calling goodnight to Mrs. Harper, and then he saw her walking quickly up the garden path, stopping once to wave back to her admirers.

He wanted to go out and speak to her—to ask if she liked his acting, to tell her that she'd been a real good Alice and that her hair was prettier than any he had ever seen. He wanted terribly to hear the good things she might have to say to him, but in spite of all that, he drew back into the shadows.

"Not yet," he thought. "Tomorrow I'll talk to her—I'll tell her for sure tomorrow."

THIRTEEN

The next day was beautiful with a bright, blue sky and a breeze that swept in from the Gulf bringing with it a welcome coolness. When Georgie opened his eyes as the sunlight brightened his room, he thought, "This is the day I'll tell her. I'll say 'Thank you for letting me be the Hatter,' and then I'll say that I like her and I wish I'd liked her a long time ago." He dreaded saying the things he knew he must. Pulling the sheet over his head, he tried to think things over, to organize his plan of action.

Over in the big green-shuttered house, Amanda was cross when she heard Robin climbing out of bed a full hour before she wanted to take up her morning duties. Amanda found it very difficult to rouse herself before eight o'clock; and to be up and around before seven seemed senseless and highly disagreeable.

"Why can't you keep quiet of a morning the way you used to do?" she asked impatiently, but a minute later her good nature overcame her irritation as Robin babbled eagerly, "Feed ducks—feed ducks."

She laughed as she swept him up in her arms and carried him into his bath. "Not for an hour or so, little pest; not till Georgie comes over. And this is Saturday when Georgie can sleep late—the way Amanda would like to do if you'd behave yourself."

When he was dressed, Robin refused to take Amanda's hand when she offered to help him down-stairs. "Robin big boy," he told her, and seating himself at the top of the stairs he proceeded to scoot down, one step at a time. When he reached the lower landing he ran quickly, if a bit uncertainly, to the kitchen and to Rosita's arms.

"Feed ducks—feed ducks," he repeated over and over, laughing and returning Rosita's hugs for a time, then growing impatient and struggling to free himself from her embrace.

"No, my precious, we can't feed the ducks unless

Georgie comes over later this morning. I'm too busy to take you, and as for Amanda—"she looked with disapproval at Amanda's wild hair and half-buttoned robe when the girl appeared—"Amanda needs to get herself combed and dressed before she's seen by anyone—even the ducks." She took a slice of bread from the bread-box and placed it in Robin's hand. "Here you are, Robin; go out in the garden and feed the pretty birds while Rosita fixes breakfast. You go with him, my lady," she added, turning to Amanda. Tell Old Eddie to come in for a roll and coffee when I ring. After you've fed Robin and had a bite yourself, I want you to get dressed before Mrs. Harper gets down—"

Amanda stretched her arms and yawned widely. "Oh, don't be so grouchy with me, Rosita. You jaw at me like you were my own mother." She grinned at Rosita and took a bottle of Coke from the refrigerator. "That Robin is gettin' to be a handful lately. Remember last year he didn't hardly make a move on his own? Now, it's all I can do to keep up with him."

Rosita watched him fondly as he trotted through the backyard toward the garden. "He's stronger—and he's learnin' any number of little things. I pray every night that some miracle—" she broke off her sentence.

From the lake road Old Eddie's truck rattled up to

the garden and parked at the gate. The old man climbed down slowly and began to unload bags of plant feed he had brought from town. He waved to Robin when he glimpsed the child's golden curls against a low green hedge near the gate.

"Hallo, there, Robin. What you doin' out here at this hour of the mornin'?" He came up to the child and lifted him high in the air. "You're gettin' bigger, Robin. I 'clare it's all I can do to raise you off the ground anymore. Your ma's goin' to have another gardener around here to help Georgie and me one of these days."

"Feed ducks," Robin babbled, showing Old Eddie the slice of bread in his hand.

"No, it's too early to feed the ducks, Robin. You wait till your partner gets over here, then you and him can give the ducks some breakfast."

Amanda came out and settled herself on one of the wrought-iron benches, taking long swallows of her pre-breakfast Coke. "Go over to the gate, Robin," she said pointing toward the south side of the garden, "go watch for Georgie. Maybe he'll be coming over pretty soon."

She hoped Georgie would come over soon. She'd turn Robin over to him after warning him loudly enough so Rosita was bound to hear, that he should take care no harm came to her little boy. After that she could go back to her room and sleep until around eleven when Rosita would probably get cranky and shoo her back to work.

Robin trotted obediently to the fence Amanda pointed out and gazed wistfully across the street toward the school. He called a few times, a garbled attempt to say Georgie, but when there was neither an answer nor an appearance of Georgie, he sighed and resigned himself to further waiting.

"Georgie sleep," he thought to himself. "Lazy Georgie sleep," he thought, and shook his head as he walked away.

Finally he wandered down to the corner where Georgie's rosebush stood, full of bloom and radiant in the morning light. He squatted beside it for a minute and before he left he patted the lower stems gently as he had seen Georgie do many times.

After a while he turned away from the south area of the garden and walked back along one of the flagstone paths. A brown toad hopped out at one point, planting itself stolidly in the middle of the path while Robin sat down in front of it. They stared at one another earnestly for a long time; then when a tiny lizard offered to join them, the toad scuttled away. Robin ran after it a little distance, awkward and uncertain as he got into some of the thick grass. He fell at last into a clump of azaleas and had a moment of difficulty in getting to his feet again and retrieving the bread he had dropped when he fell.

Amanda had stretched a great arm along the back of the bench where she sat and had leaned her head upon it. She was snoring gently when Robin stopped to look at her. Old Eddie was busily feeding hedges at the west end of the garden. In the kitchen Rosita was singing as she prepared breakfast.

Robin stood quietly, looking around him for a while, then he went over to the bird-feeder that the boys over at Georgie's school had made for his mother. He was ready to give the birds a share of the ducks' breakfast, but most of them were finding worms for themselves that morning; only two sparrows lighted on the feeder to watch for the crumbs Robin threw below. After they had grabbed a quick snack, they flew away and Robin looked after them gravely, sorry that they cared so little for him or for his gift to them.

He soon forgot the birds, however, and chased a butterfly for a few unsteady steps. Then he stopped in the area of his mother's rose garden where he buried his nose in the few blooms low enough for him to reach.

It was while he was in the rose garden that he saw the squirrel. It was frisky and quick, an impudent little creature that seemed to tease Robin as it approached him for a few steps, then waved its tail and scampered away a little distance. Robin wanted to touch it, to hold it in his hands and show it to Georgie when he finally came over to play. He followed the squirrel, laughing, but it soon got away from him, darting through a narrow opening between two ixora bushes, an opening so covered with leaves that Robin wouldn't have known it was there if he hadn't seen the squirrel run through it.

The opening was, indeed, narrow and it was all Robin could do to squeeze through it. He was caught by a tangle of branches that tried to hold him back, but he pressed on, proud to be able to do as he chose, to go into new places by himself. His thin cotton shirt was pulled over his head and left hanging in the opening; his face and arms were scratched and for a moment he was bewildered as he looked about him, the garden suddenly gone and a wide area of grass, trees, and a gravel path stretching before him.

He recognized the big gate first. It was back there that he must always wait when he and Georgie left or came into the yard—always he must wait while Georgie lifted the iron ring from a post and allowed the big gate to open. Georgie, Grandfather, Mother, Rosita, and Amanda were always careful about that iron ring.

Not until that ring was lifted could Robin ever get outside the gate and on to the sloping path that led down to the lake. Now, suddenly he was on the outside all by himself without anyone lifting the ring for him. He was able, all by himself to take the gravel path and, forgetting the squirrel, to run along laughing at his huge shadow which stayed close to him at every step. It didn't matter that he stumbled and fell occasionally; he would scramble to his feet again and run on, or stop for a minute listening to the birds who were busy in the trees throughout the meadow and into the woods.

From a distance the quail called out to him in loud, clear notes that Georgie knew how to imitate, but Robin couldn't. They were trying to talk to him, he was sure, those quail hiding in the tall grass far out in the field; they wanted to know, as Old Eddie did, what Robin was doing out so early in the bright morning.

There were other birds too, much closer than the quail. He looked up trying to see through the leaves; they could see him, he knew, because they chirped to him, talked to him in the friendly way they always did when he and Georgie walked down the path together.

"Cheep—cheep," they would say and at Georgie's urging, Robin would try to answer them. He tried again and again, so many times that finally the mocking birds began to mimic him. On this morning as he stood in the path alone, trying to see the birds in the trees above him, a mocking bird took up his words and tone. "Weep—weep," it mocked in the voice of a very little boy.

He finally reached the banyan tree where Georgie liked for him to sit quietly in the shade and listen while Georgie said lots of words. Most of the bread Rosita had given him was gone, but there was a small piece left, enough to bring the silly ducks paddling toward him when he held it out to them.

The tiny waves barely lapped at the sand along the shore; they sparkled, water and sunlight mixed together, the farthest edge of them covering Robin's feet. The water felt cool and fresh to Robin's hot feet and he stamped in it time after time, sending splashes up to his waist, making enough noise to frighten the ducks who watched him eagerly, but did not dare approach.

After a while he became aware of voices from the garden, many voices calling, "Robin—Robin—" He laughed and chortled. "Feed ducks. Feed ducks!" he cried as he stood still and held the bread out to the impatient swimmers.

Georgie always threw crumbs far out on the water and the ducks had to paddle madly away from the shore in order to get them; watching them scramble, darting in one direction and then another, sometimes fighting over a water-soaked crumb—all that was a part of the fun. But Robin was not able to throw the bread; he clutched it tightly and the eager ducks advanced toward him with hungry quacking.

They came at him from all sides, pushing against him, reaching up to peck at the bread in his hand. Robin began to be frightened. He waved his arms and tried to make them go away, but they wouldn't. They pushed against him relentlessly, and when he tried to run from them he fell face downward in the water—

FOURTEEN

During the days following the tragedy down at the lake, the big white house and the garden appeared to be running over with strangers. Georgie overheard Old Eddie talking to Sister Mary Angela about his many trips to and from the airport. "They're comin' from all over— 'specially from New York and thereabout. They got a thousand questions to put at me, but I can't talk about the little feller, Sister. I jest say to 'em, 'Missus sent me to pick you up, but I can't go over the story with you—'"

In spite of the many people coming by jet or in their own cars, there was a guarded stillness over in the garden and around the house. The same stillness had settled over the school too. Outdoor games had been abolished for the three days preceding the rites for Robin. Small groups of boys stood on the playground and looked soberly across the street talking in low voices. Sister Dolores and Sister Monica went over to Mrs. Harper's kitchen, offering their help to grieving Rosita in her task of feeding the sudden crowd of guests.

Georgie walked around the school grounds, lost to everything about him except his sorrow. Timothy tried to comfort him but Georgie shook his head silently at his friend's efforts and sat on the curb by the hour, staring across at the garden.

On the second day of stillness Sister Mary Angela called the choirboys to a meeting with her in the organ loft. "You remember a few months ago that we learned some of the music from *Hansel and Gretel*?" she asked. "Mrs. Harper heard you sing 'The Prayer' one evening— she would like for you to sing it again out at the cemetery tomorrow afternoon—"

They practiced for over an hour that morning, singing without accompaniment as they would have to sing at the cemetery. Georgie sang with them, but his throat tightened now and then as if a pair of hands closed around his neck threatening to choke the breath out of him. When the other boys left the chapel, he stayed behind to speak to Sister Mary Angela.

"Sister, I can't," he whispered. His eyes were full of agony as he looked up at her. "I can't," he repeated. "My throat is too tight—"

She took his hands and held them tightly as he stood before her. "I think you must, Georgie. Mrs. Harper loves you for your kindness to Robin. It would hurt her very much if she heard the other boys sing this last song for him and saw no Georgie among them. I think you must do this for her—"

Robin was buried in the small country cemetery beside his father and brother. The graveside rites were very simple. The choirboys sang, their voices sweet and full of tenderness for the child who had died and for his mother who watched them as they sang, unmoving and erect as she stood beside her father among their friends. Georgie sang with the others, his face so haggard that Molly Harper scarcely recognized him at first.

When the singing was over the black-robed boys were led aside by Sister Mary Angela where they stood in a quiet group for the remainder of the ceremony.

All of them, that is, but one. Georgie, unable to

bear another minute of the scene, broke away from the others and ran wildly across the brown grass and out into the dusty road. A few minutes later a car drew up beside him and one of the guests spoke quietly to him. "I am a friend of Mrs. Harper's, Georgie. She asked me to come for you and drive you back to the school." He held the car door open and Georgie reluctantly got in.

"I can't talk," he choked, remembering Old Eddie's words to the guests at the airport. The man nodded. "That's all right. None of us wants to talk right now. I'll just give you a lift home so that you can be alone—"

That evening some of the guests remained inside the house or on the porch while others walked through the garden, speaking to one another, still in the low tones of sympathy for grief. Seeing people approaching the corner of the garden where his rose grew, Georgie crawled into the shadows of the hedgerow and lay flat. He caught parts of their conversation as they passed near him.

"—severely mentally challenged, you know—hopeless—"

"—an unusually beautiful child though—"

"—surely can't stay here after this—"

"—back to New York—Hugh thinks it best for her—"

"—will take courage to go back—"

"—she can do it—Molly's strong—"

"—didn't look very strong this afternoon, poor girl—"

"—the singing—those clear, sweet voices—"

"—boy who ran away—Karl overtook him—"

"—Molly loves him—amazing that she can, after her own two—"

Gradually they drifted away, some of them going into the house for the night, others taking their cars and driving to motels outside the nearest town.

When they had all walked away, Georgie stretched himself beside his rosebush, grasping the base of it with both his arms. "I have to ask you to do it," he whispered. "I don't want to—it hurts me so bad just to think of it. But I have to ask you—" He lay on the ground, his face close to the clustered stems.

He waited until he was sure that the garden was completely deserted; then got to his feet and stole into the tool shed. In the darkness he groped along the wall from one object to another—among them a long board of soft wood in which dozens of nails had been driven loosely by an unsure hand. Robin's birdhouse, Georgie remembered. A sound broke from his throat and he stood in the darkness for a long time, holding the board in his hands. Then he searched for the spade he had come to find, and placing it in Old Eddie's smallest wheelbarrow, he crept back to his rosebush.

The task before him was awkward for the bush had grown heavier, nourished as it had been by Old Eddie's careful feeding, but the sandy soil around it crumbled easily into Georgie's spade. When the deeply bedded roots came slowly to the surface they reminded Georgie of long fingers that clung in dismay to the bed they had known for so many months. His own fingers shook as he laid the bush in the barrow with the spade beside it. Then he set out on a three-mile journey to the cemetery.

The late moon was high in the sky by the time he reached the iron gates at the entrance. They swung back easily at his first attempt to open them, but Georgie stood panting beside them, dreading to take the next few steps of his journey. He was drenched with sweat and tired to the bone. "I wish she would come looking for me—I wish she would come here and be with me," he thought. But he didn't expect that anyone knew he and the bush were gone—or that anyone would ever guess where they were. Slowly he drew off his wet shirt and threw it on the ground. It didn't matter, as he walked on toward Robin's grave, that his back was bare and that the old welts and scars showed up plainly in the moonlight.

He had just started to dig a hole for the rosebush at the foot of Robin's grave, when he heard the sound of a car approaching. A little later the car stopped at the gates and someone stood for a minute, looking through the night to the spot where Georgie stood waiting.

Finally he heard her voice. "Don't be afraid, Georgie. It's me, Mrs. Harper."

He put the spade aside and sat beside his rosebush as Molly Harper made her way through the dusty grass and finally stood before him. He looked up at her, his eyes dim with exhaustion. "How did you know where to find me?" he asked.

"Sister called to tell me you were missing—then when we found the rosebush was gone too, I hadn't any doubt. I knew you'd brought it to Robin—"

She stood looking over at Robin's grave, at the shallow hole Georgie had made at its foot, at the rosebush lying in the barrow, and finally down at Georgie's white face.

"Are you sure, Georgie?" she asked. "Are you very sure? This is a long way from the garden where you wanted it planted so much—"

"I have to do it," he answered. "We can't leave him out here by himself—he's too little—"

She took a long breath that cried softly in her throat. "Georgie, you love your bush—you'll miss it terribly. And little Robin can't—"

"I'm older now," he interrupted. "I can bear it."

"But we can buy another rosebush for Robin. You and I can go tomorrow and buy a beautiful rose for him. We can bring it out here and plant it properly in the daylight—"

He had dropped his head wearily for a minute, but now he raised it and looked at her. He wondered why she couldn't understand.

"Don't you know it wouldn't be the same?" he asked. "This is the only rosebush that Robin would love—it's the only one that's right for him. He has to have this one."

She was a long time in replying. At last she said, "You'll let me help you plant it, won't you, Georgie?"

"Yes, I wish you would help me. I guess I'm tired."

"You must be. I don't know how you managed to come so far with such a heavy load." She picked up the spade and stood looking at the hole Georgie had started. Then she thrust the spade down firmly and lifted a load of soil, depositing it to one side.

He watched her as she dug the bed for his rosebush, watched the sweat pour from her forehead and mingle with the tears on her cheeks. A question in his mind kept clamoring to be asked; the need to ask it made his eyes wide as he stared up at her.

Finally she rested against the handle of the spade for a minute, looking down at him and breathing heavily from her effort.

"Is there something you want to say to me, Georgie?"

He tried to speak but choked over his words. His eyes were full of pleading, but he shook his head after a second and then a third attempt to speak.

She knelt before him. "Tell me, Georgie, what is it you want to say to me?"

When he spoke at last his words were barely audible. "Did you born me a long time ago and I forgot?" he asked.

She looked at him for so long without speaking that he was sure he'd said something wrong, but when she placed a hand on either side of his face, he was reassured. Looking at her drawn face, he longed to comfort her.

"Sometimes I make up stories like the ones Robin's grandfather read to me at first, and I begin to think they're true. It's no matter if I'm not yours," he said.

"You are though, Georgie. I didn't 'born' you, but you're mine—no matter where I go or what I do—you're mine. Please, please, understand that—"

He glanced toward Robin's grave and at the rose-bush waiting to be planted. "Yes," he said soberly. "And if I'm yours, that's one good thing that's left—" He got to his feet abruptly and took up the spade she had laid aside. "I'm rested now. I'll do the last part of the digging."

She watched him silently as he worked and then went over to his side, helping him to lift the last spade-fuls of soil. When the bed was deep enough, they lowered the roots of the rosebush into it and pressed them firmly into their new place. Weak and tired, they stood together looking at their work.

"Old Eddie will come out tomorrow and give the bush whatever it needs," she said. She drew a hand over her wet forehead. "It's a lovely gift for Robin, Georgie."

"Yes, it's the best gift in the world." He had said that to Mrs. Sims the day he won the rosebush; it was still true tonight when he was giving it away.

Molly closed her eyes briefly at his words. Then she said, "We must go now; we must hurry back to Grandfather and Sister Mary Angela. They'll be worried until they know that we are safe."

Inside the car she turned the ignition key, but allowed the engine to run for a while without making another move. They both looked back to the place where the rosebush stood straight and tall in the moonlight, looking lonely and tired, but brave.

Neither of them spoke for a minute. Then Mrs. Harper looked down at him. "Are you ready, Georgie? Shall we go now?"

He nodded silently. As the car moved away he raised his hand and made one brief wave toward his friend. Then he drew a deep breath and turned to watch the road in front of them.